# the god & the gold

## A HAYS MCKAY ADVENTURE

### REGIS MCCAFFERTY

iUniverse, Inc.
Bloomington

**the god and the gold**
**A Hays McKay Adventure**

*This is a work of fiction. All of the characters, names, incidents,*
*organizations, and dialogue in this novel are either the products*
*of the author's imagination or are used fictitiously.*

*iUniverse books may be ordered through booksellers or by contacting:*

*iUniverse*
*1663 Liberty Drive*
*Bloomington, IN 47403*
*www.iuniverse.com*
*1-800-Authors (1-800-288-4677)*

*ISBN: 978-1-4620-0842-1 (sc)*
*ISBN: 978-1-4620-0843-8 (ebook)*

*Printed in the United States of America*

*iUniverse rev. date: 03/29/2011*

*Dedicated*
*To Violeta Roca*
*For Her Companionship And*
*Encouragement*
*And*
*To Edward Brookner*
*For His Assistance And Expert*
*Advice*

# PROLOGUE
# EVAN

Something smelled bad. Dead maybe. No... dead, certainly. It was himself. But if he was dead, how could he smell? Maybe it was a dream. Had to be a dream. No... he began to remember. It was a beautiful clear evening as usual for New Mexico, an hour before sunset, when he started across the red sandstone mesa on his way back to camp. A half hour hike would put him there about eight o'clock in plenty of time to fix a meal and transfer entries from his notebook to his laptop. When was that? Yesterday? The day before? Just then, the pain hit him. It came in waves starting with his leg and moving up through his body to his neck. He almost passed out but dragged himself back to consciousness. He vomited. Bile. Wiping his chin with his shirtsleeve, he remembered... He'd been lying in the crevasse for three days – maybe more – he'd lost track. The smell was gangrene.

Evan Begay remembered being shot. He'd been skirting the edge of the crevasse, a narrow fissure, when the shot came out of nowhere, hitting his right leg just above the knee, breaking the bone and tipping him over the edge. He'd fallen about thirty feet, hit the side and then scraped another fifteen feet along the inner face before coming to rest semiconscious, pinned on a narrow ledge. At first, he thought he'd been accidentally shot by a hunter - someone after coyote, maybe. He hollered for help but no one answered. After a few moments he thought he heard movement at the top of the crevasse and yelled again. This time there was a few seconds silence, then deep laughter, then silence again. For however long he'd been there – three days, four - there'd been no other sound. Several times, he'd written, *Help me – In crevasse*, on notebook paper, wrapped it around a rock and pitched it to the top. But they fell back to the bottom that could be seen about 80 feet below and none made it over the edge.

He wouldn't be found, or at least found in time. He knew that – felt it. He was feverish, felt faint, and was racked with pain. He slid his notebook from his jacket pocket and began to write: "I know what happened to the Anasazi eight hundred years ago; why they disappeared. It was the god and the gold..."

# Chapter 1

Bruce Hamilton walked through the door of Parker Associates, glanced at Hays McKay's office, saw it was empty and turned to Adrian Booth, staff assistant and person in charge when their boss, Ben Parker, wasn't around. "Hays been in yet?"

"No, but I had a message on my voice mail when I came in. Said he had some unfinished business to take care of and would be late. Hope he gets here soon, though, that Begay woman has called twice from New Mexico."

"A case he's working on?"

"Not that I know of. An old friend, I think."

Bruce walked to the coffee stand, poured a cup, and was just turning toward his office when Hays walked through the door. "You look none the worse for wear, Mac, considering..."

"Spent half the weekend in bed, I think."

"That's what I meant," said Bruce smiling. Hays' fiancé, Dierdre, spent the long weekend at his townhouse after he and Bruce returned from eastern Ohio and a rough time with some militia and terrorists.

Hays turned to Adrian. "Any messages?"

"A few. The boss called from Coshocton, a rather abrupt man named Theke called, and Mrs. Begay from New Mexico called twice." She handed Hays several message slips with phone numbers on them.

Hays thanked her, took them, poured himself a cup of coffee, and motioned Bruce to follow him to his office. As he sat down behind his desk, he reached out to a pipe rack, selected a large bent pipe, filled and lit it and then turned to Hamilton, smiling. "You look a little worn this morning, Bruce. Still tired from your walk in the woods?"

"Nah. Spent yesterday on a Brush-Hog clearing a quarter acre so Vivian can expand her garden. Not that we'll benefit a helluva lot from it eating wise. She wants to put most of it in flowers. What do you think Theke wants?"

"Can't imagine, but we'll call him first and find out." Hays set his pipe in an ashtray, reached for the phone and dialed the number on the message slip. A woman answered.

"Federal Bureau of Investigation, Special Branch, how may I help you?"

"Is Mr. Theke in?"

"Whom shall I say is calling?"

"Hays McKay."

"One moment please."

There was a ten second pause and then, "McKay?"

"Yes."

"As far as DOJ is concerned, you and Hamilton don't exist. Brandt will contact you."

"Well, thank..." The phone went dead. He set the phone down and looked at Bruce. "We don't exist. Son of a bitch is a man of few words."

Bruce laughed. "We knew that, didn't we?"

Hays smiled back. "Yeah, I guess we did."

Both McKay and Hamilton had been involved with Theke, an FBI team, a U.S. Marshal named Brandt, and the local Sheriff in stopping a terrorist named Ike Miller before he set off bombs in a dozen or more locations throughout the Midwest. His intentions, involving several misguided members of a local militia, were to provoke the Federal government into suspending the Constitution, or parts of it, declare martial law, and incite militia groups throughout the United States to rise up. Two members of the militia group had attempted to rape Dierdre and hadn't lived to tell about it. Nor had Ike Miller. Hays and Ike Miller's final confrontation had come in an old country church cemetery on a hill in the strip mine area of southeastern Ohio. Miller, who was wounded, told Hays to read him his rights and get him a doctor. Hays simply told him he wasn't FBI, that Miller had no rights, and that he, Hays, was his executioner. Two shots to Miller's chest ended the discussion.

"Theke said Brandt would be in touch. In the meantime, do you have any idea how we're going to account for time and expenses without giving away what we were doing there? I don't want a full report here if DOJ is going to write us out of the operation."

"Why not just 'providing assistance to local authorities' and let it go at that. Hell, local could mean Columbus or anywhere in the State."

Hays smiled. "Is being vague part of your Scottish heritage?"

Bruce laughed. "Like most Scots, I sometimes think my Scottish heritage is vague. Being devious comes naturally."

Hays was reaching for his pipe when the phone rang.

"Parker Associates, Hays McKay."

"Hays, this Anna Butler... Anna Butler Begay now. I'm living in New Mexico and I need help."

"I was just going to call you, Anna. I was out of town when you first called and only returned to the office today. What's the problem?"

"My husband Evan is missing – has been missing for almost three weeks."

"Have you contacted the local police? They should..."

She interrupted, "I contacted them the day after he was supposed to return. They investigated and even called in a search and rescue team. The team found his camp, but not Evan, and they gave up after several days searching. Didn't find any trace of him."

"I'm not sure what I can do, Anna; I'm a long way from New Mexico."

"I know, Hays, but after the local police and search teams gave up, I couldn't. He may still be alive... hurt..."

She was crying. Hays could sense it, not hear it. Softly, he asked, "How long has he been missing, Anna?"

"Three weeks yesterday."

"In New Mexico?"

"Yes, north-central New Mexico. Evan's an amateur archeologist who's been studying the

6

Anasazi culture and disappearance for years. He thought he knew where they disappeared to and why, and took a week's vacation to investigate."

"And three weeks ago was the last you saw him?"

"Saw him, yes, but he called on his cell phone early Saturday evening, the day before he was supposed to come home. He was excited. He'd found something - a gold mask and some other artifacts he didn't think were Anasazi in origin. Also some pictographs he claimed would explain where the Anasazi had gone, and why."

"Have you talked with a local detective agency, or tried to get some assistance from Indian trackers? I've heard they're good."

"The search team had trackers with them, and dogs. No luck. I contacted two agencies, one here in New Mexico and one in Texas. Both were suggested by the Sheriff's department. I'm sure they're good but both wanted fifteen hundred up front, and four hundred a day plus extraordinary expenses. I have several thousand in savings but that would be gone in about a week. I thought maybe you could..."

Hays interrupted. "I'm not sure I could do more than what's already been done, Anna. And the local people know the territory; I certainly don't. I'm not being unfeeling, it's just that I'd be working at a disadvantage. I couldn't hit the ground running."

"But I remember when we took those classes together. You had a way of looking at things... seeing thing others missed." She paused and Hays waited. "I understand if you're busy and can't take a week or so to come out here."

"OK, Anna. I'll see what assignments I have and think about it. I'll call you about six o'clock your time. That's eight o'clock here. I won't promise anything. Is that alright?"

"Oh yes, Hays, that's fine. Thank you." Her voice had perked up. "I'll wait for your call this evening."

Hays hung up, absent-mindedly reached for his pipe, lit it and turned to Bruce. "Sometimes old acquaintances come back to haunt you, or in this case, ask for help."

"I gathered that. How acquainted were you?"

Hays smiled. "Not that acquainted. Several years ago, we took some courses together at Ohio State University on southwest culture. Seems she took it to heart and moved to New Mexico. She married a Navajo named Evan Begay and he's disappeared. Search parties didn't turn up anything and for some reason she thinks I can find him when experienced trackers can't."

"You ever been to New Mexico?"

"Once. Long time ago. Drank my way across the state and vaguely remember a couple of bars on Central Avenue in Albuquerque. Central is old Route 66. Hmmm... there was a blonde in Santa Rosa too... Well, like I said, it was long time ago."

Bruce stood up. "I'd better get busy. You going to go?"

"I don't know. We're busy here, Dierdre wants to look for a house, and I'm not sure I can help. I have to think about it."

"We can get by for a week or so here if you decide to go. Might be good to talk to Ben first, though."

"Yeah, Dierdre too. By the way, she may take Ben up on his offer to come to work here as a case coordinator. I told her I not only approved but heartily endorsed it."

Bruce laughed. "And she can keep tabs on your women chasing ways as well."

"That's what she said."

"Let me know..."

"Will do."

Hays busied himself with paperwork for the next two hours, writing a concise summary of the Marvin "Ike" Miller case for Ben's personal files, and then reviewing some field reports. When he finished, he got a fresh cup of coffee, returned to his desk and relit his pipe. He'd taken several puffs and was daydreaming when the phone rang.

"Parker Associates, Hays McKay."

"Hi Parker Associates, this is Dierdre the unemployed."

"What!"

"You heard me, O love of my life – got any openings?"

"My God, honey. What the hell happened?"

Dierdre Stuart, Hays fiancé, was executive secretary to Mark Bradford, CEO and founder of Bradford Industries, and though Ben had offered her job with Parker Associates, Hays really didn't think she'd take it.

"I wasn't at my desk three minutes this morning when Mark called me into his office to tell me he wasn't happy about the amount of unplanned vacation days I'd taken lately. I said it was an unusual circumstance and in any case, I had over six weeks of accrued vacation coming. Then he went on to say he'd expect at least a week's notice in the future unless it was an emergency, started shuffling some papers on his desk, and said that was all. I was dumbfounded. Mark and I have had a great working relationship for years and it just wasn't like him at all. I just stood there. Finally he looked up and asked if I wanted something. I told him no, went to my desk and typed up a one line resignation, packed my things and left. I'm at home now."

"What did your resignation say?"

"I resign, effective immediately."

"Well, that's simple enough. He should get the message. How do you feel?"

"Upset... puzzled. The whole episode was out of character for him. Hell, Hays, you know him. He's an easy-going guy and there's never been the first problem between us. It was almost as if it was someone else talking, not Mark."

"Maybe he had a hangover."

"No – I don't think he has more than a dozen drinks a year."

"Maybe he had them all last night," said Hays, laughing.

"Dammit Mac, this isn't funny!"

"I'm sorry. You're right, it isn't. You're a key person there. I'd be surprised if he didn't call and ask you to come back."

"I won't go back. I'd almost made up my mind anyway to take Ben up on his offer if he was serious."

"He wouldn't have said it if he wasn't serious, Honey."

"Should I call him at Helen's and ask him when I start?"

"You could, but I have to talk with him anyway

and I could ask. Anna Begay called me this morning and wants me to come to New Mexico to look for her husband. I told her I'd let her know later this evening, but I'll be damned if I know what I can do that the local authorities haven't done already. Ever been to New Mexico?"

"No. Is that an invitation?"

"Depending on whether I can get away from here and when Ben wants you to start, yes."

"Call me after you talk with Ben. Mac?"

"Yeah, Honey?"

"I love you. I feel better now."

"Good. I love you too. I'll call you in an hour or so."

Hays replaced the phone, relit his pipe, and sat thinking. He didn't know Mark Bradford well but had worked a case for Bradford Industries several years before and they'd gotten along fine. He seemed affable, friendly, and had a good rapport with his employees. That was how he met Dierdre. She was his secretary even then. Dierdre was right – his behavior this morning was out of character. Could be a lot of things though: personal problems, business problems, lousy economy... At any rate, it wasn't his problem. Maybe Mark would call Dierdre later and they'd learn something. In the meantime, he'd call Ben.

Ben was staying with Helen Fishman, widow of Burgess Fishman who'd been murdered by some associates of Ike Miller. Ben was recuperating from bypass surgery and Helen had invited him to stay several weeks. Ben and Bugs, as Burgess was known in the joint, had done time together – actually shared the same cell. Bugs, a black man who had a passion for fishing, had been doing just that in an eastern Ohio strip mine area when he was killed. The guys that killed him wouldn't be harming anyone else. Hays had taken care of that. Hays punched in Helen's number. She answered on the second ring.

"Hello?"

"Hi Helen, it's Hays. Is Ben there?"

"Just came in from his walk. I'll get him."

Hays tapped the dottle from his pipe and had just set it in the ashtray when Ben said, "Hey there, fella."

"How you feelin' old man?"

"Pretty good, actually, now that the sleeping arrangements have changed for the better."

"You mean...?"

"Yeah, we're sharing the same bedroom."

"What's the doctor say...?"

"Didn't ask. Besides, she's on top. No stress." Hays heard a "Ben!" in the background and Ben laughing.

"I'm not going to pursue this topic any further," said Hays.

"Neither am I," said Ben, still laughing. Besides, I'm liable to get beat on and wind up in the hospital again."

"I'd just about bet on it. Got a couple of things to talk with you about. First is Dierdre. She wants to know if you're serious about the job as a coordinator."

"Certainly. When would she like to start?"

"Depends on the answer to the second question. A woman I knew several years ago wants me to come to New Mexico and search for her husband. Her name is Anna Begay. She's gone the official route with no luck and it's not a normal missing person situation. I told her she'd be better off with someone local but for a number of reasons, she thinks not. Bruce says there's nothing pressing for a week or so. Can you spare me for a week or ten days?"

"If Bruce and Adrian are in agreement, sure. And I suppose you want to take Deirdre with you?"

"Thought about it."

"I'll bet you did. OK, make the arrangements but stay in touch. Dierdre can go on the payroll when you get back. Is Mrs. Begay footing the bill?"

"Expenses. She doesn't have a helluva lot."

"We're not a 'non-profit' McKay."

"Yeah, I know, but the Ike Miller case didn't make us anything either." Hays knew Ben had a personal stake in stopping Miller.

"Ah shit... Yeah, well, go ahead. A week, huh?"

"Or ten days."

"OK. Wrap it up as soon as you can."

"I will, Ben. Don't eat too many of Helen's cookies."

"I could take that and run with it but I wont. Goodbye."

Hays hung up and hit the intercom button for Bruce's office.

"Yeah, Hays?"

"Lunch?"

"Sounds good. Now?"

"Yeah. Lets go to that new sandwich shop a few blocks away. I can use the walk."

"Be right there."

Over lunch, Hays filled Bruce in on his

13

conversation with Dierdre and his later one with Ben. If they could get reservations, he and Dierdre would leave for Albuquerque the following day. Leaving the sandwich shop, Hays paused on the sidewalk to light his pipe. As he did, an elderly lady stopped in front of him and watched him light it. Hays prepared for one or more anti smoking comments, but instead, she said, "That smells wonderful, young man. My husband, God love him, smoked a pipe. I always loved it."

"Well, thank you ma'am. I enjoy it too."

"Have a nice day."

"Thank you again ma'am – you too."

Bruce stepped next to Hays. "That doesn't happen very often."

"Sure doesn't. I thought I was going to be hammered for smoking on the street."

"So did I. You noticed I hung back."

Hays laughed. "Now that you mention it. Great backup you are!"

"Just playing it safe, friend – just playing it safe."

When he got back to his office, Hays told Adrian of his plans to go to New Mexico, that Ben had OK'd it, and asked her to try to get reservations for two on a morning flight to Albuquerque, but no scheduled return flight. Then he called Dierdre.

"Hello?"

"Me, Honey. Has Mark phoned?"

"Nope. I thought your call might be him. Did you talk with Ben?"

"Yep. You start when we get back. Pack a week's worth of summer clothes and head over to my place. I'm leaving here early and should be home about three unless I get hung up for some reason."

"Oh, Mac, sounds wonderful. Almost like a vacation."

"I suspect not. In fact, you may be on your own part of the time. I don't think that will happen but its hard to say at this point, so it's a play it by ear situation for now. I may know more after I talk with Anna this evening. How's pizza sound for dinner?"

"Sounds fine. Home made, or delivered?"

"Delivered. Don't want to mess with it tonight."

"What *do* you want to mess with tonight?"

"Bring something frilly that's easy for an old man to remove."

"How 'bout a towel?"

"That'll work." Hays laughed. "See ya in a couple hours."

He signed on his computer, brought up GOOGLE and typed in "Anasazi". He got almost 90,000 matches but picked one on prehistory and architecture on the first page and read for a few minutes. Much of it dealt with the Mesa Verde area in Colorado but there were several references to Chaco Canyon in New Mexico. He went back to the search engine and typed in "Chaco Canyon". He read that Chaco was one of the largest Anasazi "cities" where they'd lived for centuries, then disappeared about 1250-1300. Actually, Chaco was only one of the thousands of locations they lived in throughout Arizona, Utah, Colorado and New Mexico. For some reason, all of these people abandoned their pueblos and went somewhere. No one knows where, for certain, or why, though there are many theories. The name, Anasazi, in the Navajo tongue means, "Ancient Enemy" which is objected to by the Hopi who consider the Anasazi their ancestors, but that seemed to have more basis in legend than fact. Seeing references to several books, he jotted down the titles and authors, signed off the computer, and called the closest bookstore. Four were in stock. Thinking it unlikely they'd be gone in an hour or so, he didn't ask the clerk to hold them.

Hays slipped on his jacket, pocketed his pipe, picked up the Ike Miller file and walked to Bruce's office. Bruce was just hanging up the phone and smiled as Hays sat down. "That was Ben. He said to put your expenses on the company account and he'd figure out what to do about it when you get back. I think he figures he owes you."

"More like the other way around," Hays laughed, "but we are going to be paid something so it's probably a good idea. I brought the Miller file. Go over it when you get a chance and make changes as necessary. It's thorough enough but vague where necessary. I doubt if anyone will ever want to see it, but you never know."

"Good enough – you leaving now?"

"Yeah, gotta make a short stop on the way home. I'll call or email with contact information after I get there."

They talked for a few minutes more and Hays was getting up to leave when Adrian walked in the door with airline e-tickets and a slip of paper. "You're booked on United for 10:05 AM all the way through to Albuquerque with one change in Denver. I booked a Ford Explorer four-wheel drive for you to pick up at the airport and booked you a smoking suite at the La Quinta Inn on Menaul Road. It looked pretty close to the center of town and near the intersection of Interstates 40 and 25."

Hays took the papers and turned to Bruce. "Now we know why she's in charge of the office when the boss is out running around."

"Or laying around... no, I didn't say that," said Bruce, laughing.

"I didn't hear it." Hays turned to Adrian. "You do nice work. I'll put in a good word with Ben for you."

Adrian laughed. "After you get back, I may be doing that for you. Have a nice trip."

The bookstore was surprisingly crowded for mid afternoon and Hays, not wanting to waste time, asked a clerk to show him where he could find the books he needed. He picked three: The Book Of The Navajo by Raymond Locke, New Mexico Handbook by Steven Metzger, and In Search of the Old Ones by David Roberts. He added a map of Albuquerque, one of New Mexico, and then stood in the service line for ten minutes before putting everything on the company's charge card. When he got to his SUV, he unfolded the Albuquerque map and located Menaul Road. The address of the hotel put it just east of I-25 and north of I-40. Adrian had done a good job. He wondered how she'd managed to pick it.

Dierdre was sitting in a lawn chair at the corner of his townhouse as he pulled into the driveway and tapped the opener to raise the garage door. She was standing as he came out of the garage, took three steps forward and place both arms around his neck. "I just put a fresh pot of coffee on, or would you rather have something cold?"

"No, hot and wet is fine," he said, wrapping his arms around her waist and kissing her lightly on the lips.

"Hot and wet is later," she said, laughing.

"Shit! Where's your towel?"

"Inside. Thought the neighbors would object."

"Hell, most of them are so old, they've forgotten…"

"Not if they're anything like you."

"Hmmm…" He nuzzled her neck. "You could be right."

"OK, fella, enough for now… at least in public. What's in the sack?"

"I stopped by the bookstore on the way home and picked up some books on southwest culture and some maps. Something to look at this evening and on the plane tomorrow."

They walked into the kitchen and Dierdre poured coffee.

"What's our schedule?"

"Flight out at 10:05, change in Denver, then non-stop to Albuquerque. Should arrive about 2:PM their time. Adrian got e-tickets for us, an SUV and reservations at a midtown hotel."

"That reminds me. She phoned about ten minutes ago. Said to give her a call when you got in."

Hays set his coffee on the counter, picked up the phone and hit the autodial for the office.

"Parker Associates, Adrian Booth."

"Hi Adrian, it's Hays."

Hi Hays. I…" There was a distinct pause. "A

long time ago, I spent several months in New Mexico, mostly in Albuquerque, but traveled around the state quite a bit. I knew a Navajo named Jacob Nez who worked construction in Albuquerque nine months out of the year and was a big game guide for an outfit near the Jemez Mountains in the winter months. We've stayed in touch, kind-of... I mean maybe one letter a year and a Christmas card. His sister's a barber in Rio Rancho near Albuquerque and would probably know how to reach him. I have her address and phone number if you think someone like Jake could help in any way."

"My God, yes, Adrian! I'm going into this mess cold and have no contacts other than Anna Begay. Someone like Jacob could be a lot of help if he's willing."

"Jake – he prefers Jake. His sister's name is Jeanette and I don't think she's married, at least she wasn't last I knew."

"OK. Jake it is. I take it you knew him pretty well. Why didn't you mention this at the office?"

There was a long pause. "I had to think about it. We were very close for a short time. To be honest, Hays, a short, passionate love affair... but he had his world and I had mine. I couldn't live in his and he couldn't, or wouldn't, live in mine. We parted friends... and lovers... and I returned to Ohio. That was seven years ago."

"And you haven't seen him since?"

"Once. Five years ago, he came to the Mohegan Reservation campground near Loudonville for some sort of tribal gathering. I don't think he liked it here very much, but he was returning the favor for an Indian friend who'd been to New Mexico the year before. I stayed a couple of days..."

"I really appreciate your help, Adrian. I'll simply tell Jake that when you found out we'd be traveling to New Mexico on a case, you mentioned his name and thought he might be of some help. Other than that, I don't know a thing."

"That'll be fine, Hays. If you wrap things up early or if you have time, visit a few places out there. It's an interesting State with interesting history."

"We'll do that, and thanks again."

Dierdre looked up from the Albuquerque map. "I take it Adrian knows someone in New Mexico that could be of help."

"A Navajo named Jacob Nez. Prefers Jake. Works as a guide several months out of the year in the Jemez Mountains. I don't know if that's where we'll be going but I suspect he's familiar with a lot of different locations. Sure would be great if he can act as guide for us but we'll probably have to pay him the going rate, that is if he can cut loose from his regular job."

"What's his regular job?"

"Construction, according to Adrian."

"If he works out of a union hall, he should be able to take off when he likes. Might have to give a couple days notice but that's all."

"So how did you become such a labor expert?"

"All the work activity for the new building at Bradford Industries last year was funneled through our office for review. The crews that did the electrical and plumbing work were journeymen out of a union hall. That included the Pushers."

"Pushers?" Hays took a pipe from a small rack on the kitchen counter and began to fill it.

"Pushers are what the crews call their Foremen."

"We sure have worked in different worlds, huh? *Pusher* has a slightly different connotation in mine. When's dinner?"

"I've already ordered the pizza. Should be here in about twenty."

Between puffs while lighting his pipe, Hays said, "Efficient... little devil... aren't you? ...I think... I'll keep you around."

"I think I'll stick around, at least for a free trip to New Mexico."

Hays laughed. "Damn, and I thought the whole time it was my cooking..."

Over pizza and Pepsi, they talked more about New Mexico and looked at the maps Hays had brought. When they finished, he cleared the dishes, relit his pipe and sat down again next to Dierdre. She was looking at an area northwest of Albuquerque.

"Sure is a lot of open space with no towns or cities."

"You're right about that. New Mexico is almost four times the size of Ohio and the population is less than the Cleveland metropolitan area. I think about eighty percent is concentrated in three cities: Albuquerque, Las Cruces, and Santa Fe."

"And where was Anna Begay's husband when he disappeared?"

"She didn't say, exactly, but I suspect north and west of Santa Fe, maybe somewhere in the Jemez Mountains. If he was looking into anything

Anasazi, it would probably be there. Other than some archeology courses I took a few years back, I don't know much. Chaco Canyon, the ruins of one of the great Anasazi cities, is located there but that's about all I know. We'll have to depend on Anna and Jake Nez, if he'll help us."

He set his pipe in an ashtray, stood, and put his hand on her shoulder. "Have I got a deal for you! You do the dishes while I pack."

"Doesn't sound like a deal to me."

"OK. You pack for me and I'll do the dishes."

"That's even worse. I'll do the dishes."

Hays walked first to his den, selected seven pipes from his rack plus two he'd recently acquired: a large Peterson bent, and an Upshall billiard. He then packed a freezer bag with about a pound of tobacco he'd blended and took three tins from the drawer of his pipe cabinet. He didn't know what the pipe and tobacco situation was in New Mexico but didn't want to be caught short. He was the first to admit he was addicted to a pipe and fine tobacco blends for more years than he could count and was rarely without them. From the closet, he took a large carryon bag and went to the bedroom where he packed some clothes along with pipes, tobacco and a book on Victorian Underworld he'd been trying to read. When he got to the kitchen, Dierdre was back at the table looking at the maps.

She stood up, stretched, folded up the maps and put them in the sack with the books. "What time do we have to be at Port Columbus?"

"With all the security, I expect we'd better be there by eight."

"Taxi, or are you going to park long-term?"

"Taxi, I think. I'll call Eddie Prime. I need to call Anna too. After I call, you want to hit the rain room?"

"Oh, you got a rain room?"

"Yeah, that little stand-up area off the bedroom with overhead sprinklers. It's within leaping distance of the bed." The large bathroom with oversized shower having nozzles at both ends was one of the things that sold Hays on renting the townhouse.

"I think that pizza gave you immoral thoughts."

"I don't need pizza..."

"Call Eddie. I'll meet you in the shower."

Hays relit his pipe, picked up the phone and punched in Eddie's number. Eddie was a black, independent cab driver who was not only a friend, but a bottomless source of information about everything happening in the city, legal and illegal.

"Independent Cab – Eddie speaking."

"Hi Eddie. Hays McKay. You free tomorrow morning about seven?"

"Aw Jesus, Mac, not again!"

Hays laughed. Eddie had been invaluable on two occasions during the Ike Miller affair and had actually pointed Miller out to Hays before he had a good description. Hays had also saved Eddie from getting his throat cut.

"Not this time, Eddie. Straight forward. I need you to pick us up at my place and take us to the airport."

"Us?"

"Dierdre and myself."

"She got long legs?"

23

"We won't go there, Eddie."

"Yeah... She got long legs."

"Seven, Eddie."

"Gotcha boss, I'll be there."

He double clicked the talk button and entered Anna Begay's number. She got it on the first ring.

"Anna, it's Hays. We'll be in tomorrow, mid-afternoon. I'll call you after we get settled in at the motel, probably three o'clock or so."

"Oh God, Hays. Thank you. Are you bringing someone with you?"

"My fiancé, Dierdre. She's an investigator for Parker Associates as well, so you're getting two for the price of one." He didn't think it was necessary to go into further detail. "We'll be staying at the La Quinta Inn on Menaul. What part of town are you in?"

"The far west side near the Petroglyph National Monument. I can give you directions..."

"Not necessary now. You can tell me when I call tomorrow."

"Hays... thank you so much." The relief was evident in her voice.

"You're welcome, Anna, but don't get your hopes up too high. I'm a bit out of my depth in this instance and not sure I'll be able to learn anything you don't already know."

"I have to try, Hays."

"I know, honey, I know. I'll call you tomorrow."

Hays disconnected and headed for the bedroom, setting his pipe in an ashtray as he passed through the living room. The bathroom was already steamy as he opened the shower door.

Dierdre was standing under the spray, bar of soap in one hand and washcloth in the other, with lather running between her breasts and over her smooth stomach. He stepped in behind and up against her, wrapped both arms around her waist and then moved his right hand down between her legs. Without saying a word, he nuzzled the back of her neck. She turned to him, placed her soapy right hand between his legs and began to gently massage. His reaction was immediate. She leaned forward, and whispered, "Mr. Mac, I think I'm getting a rise out of you."

"Oh yeah, you could say that."

She laughed, turned to the spray, and quickly rinsed. "Meet you on the launching pad!" She stepped out of the shower and grabbed a towel off the rack.

"I wasn't going to wait!"

"I know."

Hays came out of the bathroom wrapped in a towel and stopped when he saw her lying on the bed, covered only to her waist with her hair spread across the pillow. He could smell the light, musky aroma of her perfume from where he stood.

She held her arms out to him and without saying a word, he went to the side of the bed. She reached out and ran her hand lightly up the inside of his leg. He dropped the towel, lifted the sheet, and moved gently next to her. They kissed... long and slow, their tongues searching, meeting.... He moved his lips downward to her breasts, first one then the other, mouthing gently as her nipples rose and became hard. He moved down farther, trailing kisses across her stomach as he slid between her legs, spread wide to receive his tongue. When he first touched her with his tongue she jerked in a small spasm and softly moaned, "Oh Mac... Mac..."

After a moment she said, "I want you in me... I want you in me..."

He moved up on top of her, hard and erect and as he entered her she let out a gasp and cried, "Oh God, yes!" And they moved together, rocking wildly, turning till she was on top of him leaning back, eyes closed, and when they both reached orgasm together, she held her breath for a moment, trembled, and then folded forward to him. After a few seconds, she gave a throaty laugh.

"To hell with New Mexico. Let's pretend we went and just stay here."

Hays ran his hand lightly down her spine. "I'd vote for that, but we're expected."

She rolled off to his right and he heard sleep in her voice. "Hmmm... if you say so. I love you..."

He turned out the light, kissed her lightly on the neck, moved to her back and put his arm around her cupping her breast. He woke in the same position when the alarm went off at 5:30.

# Chapter 2

They arrived in Albuquerque air-travel tired from the flight and hassle but happy to have only carryon bags. Their SUV was ready and after picking it up, the first thing Hays did was dig into the end pocket of his flight bag, remove two pipes, and a dashboard pipe holder. He filled one pipe and lit it, then placed the second in the pipe holder within reach while driving. Dierdre watched this exercise with a smile on her face.

"Important things first, huh? Didn't even check if there was gas in this monster or if the brakes work. I'm surprised you don't have one of those pipe holders mounted on the headboard of your bed."

"Thought about it."

"I'll bet you did!"

"Would have done it too, but had visions of a hot pipe falling onto an important part of your anatomy during the action. Course, I could dress you in asbestos..."

"Shit!"

"Yeah... well... that's what I thought."

He took several puffs as he fastened his seatbelt, adjusted the rearview mirrors, and then headed out of the parking garage to the motel. Just as Adrian told him, the hotel was only fifteen minutes from the airport on Menaul, just off University Boulevard and nearby access to both major interstates. They checked in and started pot of coffee while putting their clothes away. He poured them both a cup of coffee while she used and checked out the fixtures in the bathroom, and was sitting on the bed, holding his mini notebook computer in one hand and pipe in the other when she came out looking fresh and combed.

She stopped at the end of the bed. "With both hands full, are you going to lap up your coffee or do you want me to call room service for a straw?"

"Cynicism, that's what I love about you."

"That all?"

"Gimme a little time and I might think of something else."

She took two quick steps, grabbed a pillow and swung as he rolled to the other side of the bed, narrowly being missed by the solid *thump* behind him.

"Damn," he said, moving back around the bed to the phone, "vindictive too. There goes my idea of picking up some nice New Mexican girl..."

This time she threw the pillow in a flat trajectory that caught him full in the face and he fell back on the bed laughing. She jumped onto the bed next to him, put one hand on his crotch and nuzzled his neck.

"But I have my hands full, wench!"

"So do I." She was laughing too but after a few seconds rolled off the bed and picked up her coffee. "I suppose you want to call the woman who brought us here."

"She'd probably appreciate it." He picked up his phone and entered the speed dial number. Anna picked up on the third ring.

"Hello?"

"Anna, It's Hays. We're at the hotel. If you can give me some directions, we can be at your place in a half hour or so."

He scribbled a few lines on the pad by the phone, said goodbye, and handed the paper to Dierdre while heading for the bathroom with a comment about a pit stop. When he came out, he slipped on his long travel vest, put two pipes in one pocket and a tobacco pouch in another.

She watched him with a grin. "What would you do, Mac, if they ever stopped making tobacco?"

"Grow my own."

"And if they made it illegal?"

"Grow my own."

"Pretty single minded on that point, aren't we?"

"A pipe and good tobacco have been one of the great pleasures and satisfactions in my life for more years than I care to remember. I think I'll leave instructions in my will to be packed in a good blend when they cremate me."

"Are you serious?"

"Hadn't given it any thought till you brought it up." He was smiling now. "I can just picture that blue-white smoke coming up from the crematorium, and the great aroma of a fine blended Virginia tobacco."

"Oh Lord, I'm 1800 miles from home with a wacky Irishman."

"I'll let you whack my Irishman later. Right now, we're headed west."

They found the entrance ramp to I-40 West with ease and within a few minutes exited north at Unser Boulevard. As they drove, they could see the volcanic escarpment to their left, rising in some places over 300 feet to a mesa. After traveling four miles they came to the intersection they were looking for, turned left and followed the street to the first cul-de-sac. Hays turned left and drove straight to the adobe style house at the end of the street. As they pulled in the driveway, Anna Begay came out the front door. She hadn't changed much from what Hays remembered; still attractive and slender, but her shoulder length, deep chestnut colored hair showed streaks of gray that she didn't try to hide. It was actually quite appealing.

She walked past Hays and smiling, held out her hand to Dierdre. "Hi, I'm Anna, one of Hay's old school chums."

Smart woman, thought Hays, but said, "Hey old school chum, I'm over here."

"I saw you but thought I'd greet the boss first." She moved to Hays, gave him a hug and then turned toward the house. "Let's go to the patio in back. I have cold, hot, and sandwich stuff if you're hungry."

The back yard was large, angular, surrounded by a six-foot wooden fence, and desert like in appearance with no grass. There were several large volcanic boulders at strategic locations, surrounded by small pink colored stone, with cactus and other desert plants in a random pattern in the remaining yard which was mostly sand. Very nice and very southwestern, thought Hays as he took a seat in a comfortable, canvas lawn chair. Anna brought out a large tray with Cokes and sandwiches and sat it on the table between them.

Dierdre took a sip of her drink and looked out over the yard. "I noticed almost all the homes here are fenced. We don't see much of that in Ohio."

"It's called a coyote fence, and meant to keep coyotes out," said Anna, "though in southwest cities, its as much tradition and decoration as anything. Here on the west mesa and in the Bosque along the Rio Grande it does help keep them out of the yard, though I dare say they could dig under it if they had a mind to. Sometimes they do and the family cat becomes an item on their menu. They're mostly night hunters and sometimes make a lot of noise yodeling and yelping as a pack makes its way along the fences that border the volcanic escarpment here. Sets off every damn dog in the neighborhood, usually at some ungodly hour like two in the morning."

Hays set his sandwich down and moved his arm in an arc toward the huge volcanic boulders that jutted out of the escarpment and littered the base of the slope. "This is all part of the Petroglyph National Monument, isn't it?"

"Yes. It runs for about seven miles north and south and from several hundred yards, to almost a mile wide."

"I know what pictographs are," said Dierdre, "but what are Petroglyphs?"

"The idea is about the same, though pictographs are generally more colorful and artistic. Pictographs are wall paintings, usually found in caves or protected areas, whereas petroglyphs are symbols, figures, or other representations carved in rock, usually volcanic, and usually outside in the weather." Anna pointed up to the escarpment. "I think the Park Service has identified over ten thousand in this area but there are probably double that number. Just haven't been spotted yet." She paused. "That's what Evan spent most of his time studying. He seemed to think the answer to the disappearance of the Anasazi would be told in some drawing or rock carving somewhere, but that no one had found it yet."

Hays had finished his sandwich and fished in his pocket for a pipe. "Do you mind if I smoke?"

Anna smiled. "No, not at all. I like a pipe. Evan has... had a couple but he preferred cigars, though he didn't smoke them often."

Hays filled and lit his pipe, tamped the ash, and relit it. "So Evan had taken a vacation to look for some clue in the disappearance of the Anasazi. Two questions come to mind. Did he do that often? And did a lot of people know about it?"

"Yes to both. He'd been with his company for a long time and had a lot of vacation built up. Not only that, but at least one weekend a month he'd drive to Chaco Canyon or some other known Anasazi site just to look around, or as he put it, get a feel for the Puebloan Indians who lived there. He talked about it to anyone who would listen. I wouldn't call it a consuming passion, but it was a passion for him. There are almost as many theories of why the Anasazi disappeared as there are Archeologists who study them. Evan didn't believe... I guess it would be better to say he didn't subscribe to most of them, at least the most popular ones. The theory at the top of most lists is that drought drove the Anasazi toward the Rio Grande, but Evan would laugh and say it didn't hold water. He said it didn't explain why they disappeared from all the other areas, some hundreds of miles west and south, at the same time. And if they did migrate to the Rio Grande, why aren't thousands of Anasazi artifacts found along the river? He thought if drought forced them to move from the Chaco Canyon area, they would have simply moved east about 60 miles into the Jemez Mountains where some small bands of Anasazi were already living. Plenty of game, decent soil, and water. That's the area he'd been concentrating on for the past year and where he was when he disappeared."

Hays was puffing slowly on his pipe and staring at the volcanic escarpment. "So what do you think happened, Anna? I can't imagine some scientist wanting to do him harm simply because he stumbled onto proof behind their disappearance. And we still can't rule out some accident, though you'd think his body would have been discovered in the search."

"I don't know, Hays, I truly don't. But he was a cautious man and beyond that, he was in his element outdoors. I don't believe he had an accident."

"What if," said Dierdre, "he stumbled onto something valuable. Not valuable in the archeological sense, but in a more modern sense. Because of who he was and his passion for the Anasazi, we seem to be concentrating on that. It may well be that his search put him in that area, but his disappearance might not have anything to do with it. Maybe we should take a clue from his own suspicion of obvious theories regarding the disappearance of the Anasazi and apply it in this case."

Hays took the pipe from his mouth, looked at Dierdre and then turned to Anna. "Now you know why she's here. And she's right, of course. If we eliminate accident and anything related to an archeological discovery, at least in the scientific sense, then we're left with what may well be a modern crime for modern reasons. The two most common are love and money, which leads me to a question no investigator likes to ask but has to. How would you describe your relationship with Evan?"

"The police asked the same thing and I expected you would too. I loved him deeply and believe in my heart he felt the same way, though he didn't express it as much outwardly as I may have. He was Navajo. Public displays of affection weren't his way, but in private... Let me put it this way: the Anasazi weren't his only passion." She blushed and Hays could see tears weren't far off. He set his pipe on the table.

"Alright then, Anna, we're going to need some things. Did Evan have any maps of the area he was looking into? Also, did he keep notes – something on a computer maybe, or even by hand? We need a starting point, a physical location, but in addition to that, we need to know what area has already been searched."

"I have all that and more. He kept meticulous notes on his desktop computer and I have maps showing areas he was looking into, where he was camped, and where the Sheriff's department searched. I thought you'd need them, so I put it all together. Along with a small paper notebook, he had a small laptop he'd take to the field and then transfer notes to his desktop. I downloaded his notes to a CD and there's an index that goes with it. Is there anything else?"

"Firearms. Did Evan own any guns or do you have any? Trying to transport firearms on an airplane in this day and age is a hassle. We didn't bring any with us."

"I have a house gun I keep loaded in a table next to the bed, but Evan was a hunter and had several, though he hasn't hunted much in the past few years. He took a rifle with him and a handgun. We'll have to look in his gun safe. He also had a concealed carry permit he got about a year after the law was signed by the Governor. Let's go inside, take a look in the safe and I'll get the information I put together for you."

Inside, they went to a den that doubled as library and computer room. There were maps of the southwest on the wall, many with hand-highlighted areas and notes scribbled on them. The gun-safe was large, with double doors and sat in a corner. Anna handed two large envelopes to Dierdre saying they contained notes, maps, and the CD's she'd downloaded, then turned to the gun safe and worked the combination.

Evan had firearms, alright: four rifles, three handguns, and four shotguns, including an old external hammer model 97 Winchester pump in 12 gauge. All were well used but clean and meticulously cared for. The three handguns were revolvers, two in .357 magnum and one .22, all Smith & Wesson. Hays picked up one of the rifles.

It was a Ruger #1 dropping block, single shot, in 45-70 caliber with a 3X9 variable scope. He worked the action. It was smooth as silk.

"That rifle was Evan's favorite. He took three Elk with it over the years, all with a single shot and all at about 200 yards. He said it had tremendous knock down power and I shot it once. He was right – it almost knocked me down." Anna smiled, remembering. "There is one other rifle, a Marlin lever action the Sheriff's Department has but they said they'd be returning it this week. They found it at Evan's camp but didn't find the .38 he also had with him. I expect he was carrying it. The Marlin is the same caliber as the single shot."

"We'll borrow two rifles, two handguns, and a shotgun, and take them with us back to the hotel." Hays tamped and relit his pipe, thinking. "Better go heavy and light. We'll take the Ruger, the .243 bolt action, .357 and .22 pistols, and the old Winchester shotgun. We have a Navajo tracker to contact yet today if we can. If he's free, we can get started day after tomorrow and move to the Jemez Mountains. Is there a camper or trailer rental nearby?"

"There's one in Rio Rancho about 20 minutes from here. Are you actually going to move there?"

"Yes. We'll set up a camp in the mountains so there's no need to keep the hotel room."

"You know a Navajo tracker here? How is that?"

"We don't actually know him. Not yet anyway. He's a friend of a friend back in Ohio and was recommended as someone who lives in and hunts the Jemez Mountains. At least he lives there part-time. I think he works in Albuquerque or around the State several months out of the year and then guides for a hunting lodge during the season. It was suggested we get hold of him and see if he's free for a week or so."

"Will he be expensive?"

"I don't know. But don't worry about cost now. He'll be paid out of agency funds and we'll figure it out later. The important thing now is to find Evan and determine what happened. OK?"

"OK." She was crying now and Dierdre stepped forward to put her arm around her, turning Anna to her.

"Hays is like a pit bull, Anna, he won't let go of a problem once he gets hold of it. Between tenacity and that crazy intuitive logic he has, we'll find something." Dierdre looked at Hays. Left unsaid was that it was entirely possible they wouldn't like what they found.

Hays packed the guns in cases he found in the bottom of the gun-safe and then slipped them into a large duffle that was on the floor of the safe. He put them in the SUV and after telling Anna they'd be in touch in the morning, they returned to the hotel. In the time it took him to carry the guns into the suite and put them in the closet, Deirdre had started going through the information Anna had given them. She separated it into three small piles: maps, notes, and CD's. Some of the notes were computer printed while others were hand written.

Hays opened his pipe case, removed his new Upshall Billiard and a large roll-up pouch of Samuel Gawith Best Brown Flake tobacco.

He filled the pipe, lit it and took several puffs before setting it in an ashtray. "Tell ya what: why don't you take a look at the notes while I sort through the maps to get a feel of where we might be headed. If I'm going to ask Jake Nez to lend a hand, I should be able to give him some idea of the general area. Afterwards, or maybe after dinner, we can look at the CD's together."

Dierdre picked up the notes, propped two pillows against the bed headboard and after getting comfortable, laid the pile of notes in her lap. "I suppose this is what you call division of labor. You look at a half dozen maps and I go through a three-inch stack of notes. Damn, there must be 200 pages here."

"That's OK, it'll keep your mind off sex."

"How the hell did you know..."

"Because that's what I'm trying to do."

"My God, Mac, you can't be horny!"

"Like an Irishman with a bottle of Old Bushmills in one hand and a jug of Viagra in t'other."

"And just what are you going to be like in another 30 years?"

"Like an Irishman with a jug of Viagra in both hands."

They both laughed and then went to the job at hand. Hays sat on the edge of the bed with the first map spread out before him. It was a map of Indian Territory and identified the Reservations located in New Mexico, Arizona, Utah and Colorado. Though of little help with their present task, the Anasazi sites Evan visited had been inked in and then highlighted in orange marker. Overall, it covered hundreds of thousands of square miles. New Mexico alone was over 120,000 square miles, much of it uninhabited even today. One New Mexico county, Harding, was over four times the size of Franklin county in Ohio where Columbus was located, but where Franklin county had a population of over a million, Harding had a population of less than 800. Lots of room to wander, thought Hays. But overall, the map painted a panoramic picture of how widespread the Anasazi culture was and he could begin to understand Evan's fascination with their disappearance.

The second map had been pieced together from two sections. Topographical, and in greater detail with contour and elevations, it covered an area in New Mexico from just west of Chaco Canyon to Bandolier near the eastern edge of the Jemez Mountains and present day Los Alamos. What looked like a path or route running from Chaco Mesa east to an area north northeast of the town of La Cueva, between San Antonio Mountain and Redondo Peak, had been penciled in and highlighted. At one point along the route, Evan had written, **Four days at most – even with belongings**, and Hays assumed that meant travel time. Perhaps Evan had actually walked it. At one point just south of San Antonio Mountain, he'd penciled in, **Check the Mesa, look in caves**, and a date that corresponded with the week of his disappearance. Well, it was a starting point.

Absentmindedly, he reached for his pipe, lit it, picked up his cell phone and looked up the phone number Adrian had given him for Jeanette Nez. When he found it, he hit the call button and waited. A woman answered on the fourth ring.

"Hello?"

"Is this Jeanette Nez?" Hays set his pipe in the ashtray.

"I don't buy anything over the phone."

"Don't hang up! I'm not selling anything. I'm from Ohio and my name is Hays McKay. Adrian Booth gave me your phone number."

"Adrian? I haven't talked with Adrian for a long time. How is she?"

"She's just fine. She's the office manager for a security agency in Columbus. I work for the same agency and am here on a case that may take me to the Jamez Mountains. She thought your brother Jacob might be able to help but she didn't have his phone number so she gave me yours. Do you have Jacob's number?"

There was a pause of maybe ten seconds but Hays didn't press it. Finally, she said, "They were very close at one time, Jake and Adrian. Don't know as they've talked with each other for a while, though. You give me your phone number and I'll tell Jake this evening. Tell him you'd like him to call about eight. That OK?"

"That would be fine, and I really appreciate it. Thank you." He gave her their phone number and clicked off.

He looked at Dierdre. "Wary. Guess I can't blame her. She doesn't know me from Adam – or General Custer, for that matter."

"Boy, is your view of history screwed up. Wrong General, wrong State, wrong Indian Nation. Now, if you would have said Jim Bridger..."

"Bridger? I thought he was a mountain man and scout."

"He was, but made his home in northern New Mexico. For the most part he was a friend to the Indians, but he conducted a major military campaign against the Navajo late in his life. They never forgave him."

"So when did you become a historian of the southwest?"

"On the airplane on the way here. You gave me the book, remember?"

"I guess I should have read it first."

"Wouldn't hurt. Maybe if I hide your Viagra tonight, you'll find time."

"Maybe if I had some Viagra, I'd give it to you to hide, but what you're saying is a good idea. Might be worth an hour's reading this evening. In the meantime, we have a few hours to kill. She said she'd ask Jake to call about eight o'clock. What do you say about taking a walk in about an hour and finding some place to eat?"

"Sounds good. Someplace Mexican, maybe. I'll call the front desk and ask if there's someplace close-by."

Hays went back to looking at the topo map but wasn't really seeing it. He was wondering if it would be wise to contact the Sheriff's Department in Sandoval County. They'd conducted the search for Evan. He might learn something that could be helpful, but suspected they'd be reluctant to pass along much information. There was still the possibility this wasn't an accident and aside from that, he and Deirdre were outsiders. Best not to open that door for now, he decided – maybe later.

Dierdre had just hung up the phone. "There's a place about two blocks east that has good Mexican food. At least that's according to the fellow on the front desk. Want to give it a try?"

"Sure, why not? In the meantime, I've found some notes on one topo map that will give us a starting point, I think. Find anything in his notes?"

"Some interesting background on the Anasazi in his own words. He's a good writer. Not only that, I have a sneaking suspicion you two would have liked each other. He was analytical, imaginative, and used a lot of common sense. Listen to this:

*I'm aware that many, if not most Archeologists who have studied the Anasazi, subscribe to the theory of mass migration toward the Rio Grande estuary as the result of prolonged drought – at least for those Indians who lived in the Chaco Canyon area. I'm not an Archeologist, at least not in the formal sense, but for years, I've studied the Anasazi culture in addition to the Cohonia, Hohokam, and Mogollon cultures of Arizona, New Mexico, and the Colorado Plateau. To my mind, the disappearance of these geographically widespread cultures, all at roughly the same time, and sometimes abruptly, cannot be explained by lack of water. In addition to that, no culture migrates from one area to another without taking the makings of their culture with them. If they've been making bowls, pots, clothes, baskets a certain way for over a thousand years, they don't change all those identifying features simply because they shifted locations by a hundred miles or so.*

*I am Navajo. Being Navajo doesn't mean I have any direct relationship to the Anasazi. In fact, the Athapascan Indians (Navajo and Apache) didn't migrate to the Arizona-New Mexico area till about 1300 AD, at least 100 years after the Anasazi*

*disappeared. There is something, however... Call
it a mythical sense of being, or feeling of kinship,
if you will, but I sometimes feel as though I'm with
the Anasazi and the clock has been turned back
800 years. This feeling is never stronger than
when I'm walking in the footsteps of these ancient
puebloans, living outdoors and wandering through
areas where they once lived. And that's why, if
you'll pardon the pun, I don't believe in the theory
of migration as a result of drought – it doesn't hold
water.*

*If I were an Anasazi leader and wanted to
abandon Chaco because of lack of water, I wouldn't
move my people as far as the Rio Grande. I'd simply
move east about 60 miles to the Jemez Mountains,
near and above an area of what today is called
the Valles Caldera. Water, snowmelt, plenty of
game and good soil. But in fact, there were already
families of Anasazi living in the Jemez Mountains
and they disappeared as well. Bandolier is a case
in point and the cave dwellings there are not far
from two rivers and natural impound water in the
mountains.*

Hays relit his pipe and took several short puffs.
"You're right – I would have liked him. That's an
intelligent and thoughtful piece. Is there more?"

"Quite a bit, but few are dated. What does have
a date, I'm trying to put in order. Some of these
are computer printouts and some handwritten.
If we find them, or at least some of them, on the
CD's we can probably date them if we have a need
to."

They continued for another half hour, then
left the room to walk several blocks to a small

Mexican restaurant where Dierdre was introduced to and fell in love with sopapias, a light pastry-like pocket filled with chicken, lettuce, cheese, and topped with green chili. Hays had the same and they both had an O'Doul's Amber with it.

Dierdre took a sip of her beer and looked at Hays. "Does it ever bother you not to drink any *booze*, booze?"

"You mean alcoholic stuff. No, not really. Not any more. Years ago, maybe, but in the case of beer, I never drank much of it anyway. Maybe one with a meal and that was enough. Now scotch, on the other hand... I could just pop the top and put a straw in the bottle."

"Back in the good old days, huh?"

"Some were, but they were damned few and far between, particularly at the end of a long alcoholic slide downhill. No one saved my butt – you can only save your own – but Ben gave me hope and direction; helped pull me back to humanity. He was always there. I once told him I could never repay him. He said, sure you can – just reach your hand out to another suffering alcoholic, that's payment enough... And that's what I've done when I've had the chance, which hasn't been often, lately. Maybe I'll get to some meetings when we get back. Share some of my wit and wisdom."

"And twisted sense of humor as well, no doubt." She was smiling. "I sure do love you, Mr. Mac, but you do tend to intrude on my nice, quiet, sedate life. Think about it – Here I am, over 1700 miles from my apartment in Ohio, preparing to traipse off into the wilderness replete with lions and tigers and bears and such, searching for a searcher who probably fell into a hole somewhere. Either that or maybe he just decided to disappear, pull the plug, move to Kansas and search for Dorothy and Toto."

"Ah, me love, this old Irishman has been accused of being cynical, but I think you just moved to the head of the class. You don't really believe any of that shit do you?"

"No, but as Sherlock was fond of saying, when you have excluded the impossible, whatever remains, must be the truth. I don't think we should exclude anything. In fact, we don't know enough to exclude anything. The only thing we know for sure is that Evan Begay didn't show up for dinner as planned."

"Now you're being facetious."

"True, but think about it. We're going charging off into the wilderness and for all we know, he could be staying in the room next to us."

Hays looked at her for a few seconds and then fished in his pocket for his pipe to smoke on the way back to the hotel. "Know what I like about you?"

"What?"

"Sex. You really turn me on."

"Now you're being facetious!"

"Yep – but it's true. Also true is what you're saying. We can make educated guesses based on what we know or think we know, but they are only guesses - conjecture and no more. But to begin somewhere, we have to make assumptions. We will assume the information we have from Evan, through his writing and notes, is the foundation for his excursion to the Jemez Mountains. His disappearance, however it came about, and for whatever reason, is real. We have nothing that tells us whether it was accidental or intentional. If intentional, it seems unlikely that Evan initiated it, though as you say, we can't rule that out. You want a gut feeling? I think he was murdered."

"My God, why do you say that?"

"Gold, me love, gold. Didn't Anna say he'd found a gold mask? Perhaps there's more than just a mask. Melted down, gold brings a nice price, but a mask that's potentially 800 years old could well be worth millions to a private collector. Even more so if it explains the disappearance of an ancient culture. Evan's a well-known amateur archeologist and I'll bet people who live in the area know him and what his mission in life is. His nature and culture wouldn't permit him to profit by what he found. He'd turn those artifacts over to a museum, but believe me, he's in the minority."

"I hope you're wrong – about murder, I mean. An accident is something one can cope with, but murder...? She glanced at her watch. "We'd better be getting back. Its about twenty to eight."

The evening was cool and beautiful with the setting sun turning a few scattered clouds from pink to pale orange with the reflection falling on the slopes of the Sandia Mountains to the east. The sweet smell of flowers that had been planted around the hotel permeated the air. Dierdre gave a chuckle as she walked into the hotel entrance in front of Hays.

"What's so funny?"

"I was just thinking how nice it would be to live here and then the thought occurred to me that you might like to ask Ben if he'd like to open an

Albuquerque branch of Parker Associates. Not!" This time she laughed aloud.

"No… But I might."

She stopped so abruptly Hays ran into her, sending her flying forward to be stopped only by the front desk.

The clerk looked up. "Can I help you, ma'am?"

"Don't mind me, I just had the hottest hot flash of my life."

"Ma'am?"

Hays was at Dierdre's elbow and turned to the clerk. In a beautiful Irish brogue he said, "Aye, laddie. Going through the change, doncha know. Stumbles a lot when they come on her like that. Barmy sometimes too."

"Shit!" Dierdre kicked him in the shin.

"See what I mean? Poor lass doesn't know what she's doing." Hays was moving down the hallway out of kicking range, laughing as he went. Over his shoulder he said to the clerk, "She'll be alright as soon as she gets to the room and in a prone position."

"God is going to get you for that, McKay. And if he doesn't, I will!"

The phone was ringing as they entered the room and Hays sat down on the edge of the bed as he picked it up.

"McKay."

"This is Jake Nez. My sister said you wanted to talk with me."

"Mr. Nez, I'm from Ohio, but I'm here in New Mexico looking into the disappearance of Evan Begay a few weeks ago. His wife Anna is an old friend of mine. Adrian Booth, who is also a friend, suggested I get in touch with you. Said you were familiar with the Jemez Mountains."

There was a few seconds silence. "How is Adrian?"

"She's just fine. She's the office manager of the agency I work for and told me to be sure to tell you she said hello."

Another pause... "She married or anything?"

Hays didn't want to go there, not right now anyway, but said, "No – not married, and as far as I know, not dating anyone either." He picked up his pipe from the nightstand and lit it.

"I read about that Begay fella in the paper... Think I met him once in a little store near Fenton Lake. Never found him, did they?"

"No. That's the reason we're here."

"We?"

"Myself and another investigator."

"Must be some hot shit if they send two of you."

"Could be. Seems Evan Begay may have stumbled onto something valuable in addition to being archeologically important."

"Like what?"

"Could we get together, Mr. Nez? We need a guide and I'm willing to pay the going rate that you'd get during hunting season."

"Jake – Everyone calls me Jake. There's a Village Inn on the west side of Coors Bypass just past the Intel factory in Rio Rancho. I can meet you for coffee tomorrow morning... say nine o'clock. That OK?"

"That's fine. We're at the La Quinta on Menaul. How far is that from the Village Inn?"

"About 30 minutes or a bit less. Take I-25

north to Passeo del Norte, then west on Passeo about five miles to Coors. North on Coors about three miles. Stay in the middle lane till you get to Intel."

"How will we know you?"

"I'll be the biggest Indian in one of the booths. How will I know you?"

"My partner has auburn hair and is built like a brick shithouse."

"Yeah – that oughta do it.

"See you tomorrow morning, Jake... and thanks."

"Welcome."

Dierdre was sitting at the table looking at him. "Built like a brick shithouse?"

"It was all I could think of at the time. You know, firm, good angles, pointy things in the right places..."

She literally leaped from the chair to the bed, bowling Hays over on his back, and grabbed him by the crotch. "How would you like to be referred to as *The Soprano* or S*queaky* for the rest of your life?" They were both laughing but she didn't let go. "I mean it. I don't like that brick shithouse description. And since I have you by the balls so to speak, what did you mean when you said you might open an agency here?" She released him and they both sat up on the edge of the bed.

Hays brushed a few flakes of tobacco ash off his shirt. "I'd forgotten how beautiful the southwest is, at least to me. High desert, clean air, mountains, wildlife, large uninhabited spaces... I make jokes about drinking my way across Arizona and New Mexico years ago and to a large degree, its true. But I wasn't drunk the whole time..." He paused and put his arm around her. "I think it's a place I'd like to live – a place we'd enjoy together. Maybe a great place for a ranch with a few horses, dogs..." His voice trailed off.

"You're really serious, aren't you?"

"It's something to think about. It would take a lot of planning, several visits, and most of all, money. Then there's always Ben. The one thing I won't do is cut him off at the pass if he needs me, but if you like the idea, we can think about – talk about it more when this case is dealt with. In the meantime, we need to get back to the material we have and put it in some order. I want to look at these maps again. Maybe you could take a look at the CD's and see if there's something we can use."

# Chapter 3

For the next two hours they concentrated on the task at hand, Hays finally setting aside the maps to help Dierdre sort through the additional printed material and as much as possible put papers in date order. In some cases, it was time consuming because they had to scan the text for content to get a feel for when it was written.

Finally, Deirdre picked up the stack of papers and CDs and set them on the table. "Would you like to smoke a pipe on the balcony?"

Hays smiled and reached for his pipe. "Do I sense an ulterior motive?"

"Yes... and kind of a serious one, at least to me."

They moved to the balcony where Hays lit his pipe and sat down. "OK. I'm ready for a serious question."

Deirdre turned her chair so she was facing Hays. "We're going to be married soon and you know just about all there is to know about me but there's a part of you, a time in your life, that I know nothing about."

"And a woman, too."

"Yes, and a woman, too. You haven't exactly refused to talk about what happened in Pakistan and England some years ago and when the subject came up, you always seemed to deftly maneuver us to another subject."

"Like Amsterdam linguini."

She smiled. "Like Amsterdam linguini. Would it bother you too much to talk about it?"

Hays drew on his pipe and stared off in the distance toward the Sandia Mountains. "No, and it's a fair question. Dredging up old memories, particularly painful ones, isn't easy, but for you, I'll do it... For us, I'll do it."

"I was in Pakistan as a sniper with a small unit, working under contract to a US agency who shall remain nameless. Our mission was to take out, kill if you like, certain leaders of Al Qaeda who operated on both sides of the Pakistan-Afghan border. We lived and dressed the part. A couple of our group spoke Pashto, also known as Afghani, and a couple, including myself, spoke some Punjabi. We operated mostly in the Northwest Territories north of the large city of Peshawar and every few weeks we'd return for a few days rest at one of the Pearl Continental hotels in that city.

"That was where I met Ayesha. She came from a well to do family and had an excellent education, having spent two of her college years in France. She spoke several languages very well, including English with a British accent. She held a government liaison post and though it didn't involve direct contact with our unit, she was part of the Pakistani group who met with members of our consulate staff.

"She and I hit it off immediately. We enjoyed each other's company and as often as possible had lunch or dinner together. One thing led to another and we became lovers. In secret, of course. The Pakistan government frowns on such things and in fact, opposes marriage between Americans and Pakistanis. It's not an outright ban but they make it all but impossible for a marriage to take place in Pakistan between a non Pakistani man and a Pakistani woman. I was never told there was a religious connection but because Pakistan is a secular Islamic country, it's probably a good assumption. In addition, there was always the legitimate concern that the man would return to his home country and leave his wife, and children if they had any, in Pakistan to fend for themselves. Their culture frowns on divorced women and even more-so on those who have been abandoned.

"Six months or so went by and then Ayesha got word that she would be sent to France for two weeks for a conference of some sort. As it happened, my tour was up at about the same time and I received permission for two months leave of absence. We made plans. Oh, I suppose there were big gaping holes in them but we were in love and anything seemed possible. I arrived in Paris three days after Ayesha and booked a room at the same hotel, the Novotel Paris Les Halles, within walking distance of the Seine and the Louvre.

"She had applied for and received a visitor's visa for England. We had it in our heads if we could simply keep moving west, we'd somehow make it to America and everything would be alright. We booked a flight for London on Wednesday of the following week, her second scheduled week in

Paris and two days before she was to return to Pakistan. It went off without a hitch. We arrived in London and at the recommendation of our cab driver, checked into a small hotel about one block off Bayswater Road near Hyde Park. Within two days, we had gotten into the habit of one of us going to a small shop near Marble Arch for coffee, scones, cheese and fruit, and bringing it back to the room for breakfast.

"One morning, about a week into our stay, Ayesha had taken a shower before I did and said she'd get breakfast for us. Fifteen minutes later I had just stepped out of the shower when I heard and felt the blast. I'd been around such things too long not to know what it was. A bomb, and not far away. I dressed hurriedly and waited for Ayesha to return but after twenty minutes, decided to head for Marble Arch, hoping to see her coming back to the hotel."

Hays paused, took a deep breath, tamped and relit his pipe, and then went on. "They told me she suffered not at all. Couldn't have. She had just come out of the shop and was walking past a car when it exploded. Seven others were killed in addition to the driver. It was accidental. The bomb was being transported to another location and wasn't intended for detonation near Marble Arch. Four members of a radical IRA group were implicated, the driver and three others who weren't in the car but were in London. But not for long. By the time the police had identified the driver a day later, his known associates had flown the coop. The police were certain they'd returned to Ireland but where and how, they didn't know.

"I was numb, in a fog. I didn't even feel rage

- that would come later. After hearing my story and that we intended to be married, a detective inspector with New Scotland Yard took pity on me and made arrangements for Ayesha's remains to be buried in a cemetery just outside London. I left London for Dublin and then to Inishbofin, called the island of the white cow, off the coast of Ireland where I lived in a stone hut and stayed drunk for a month. I finally came to my senses, or thought I did, and returned to Dublin where I got a room in a bed and breakfast and sobered up enough to contact several friends inside the agency and out. Within twenty four hours they provided me with the names of the IRA cell that had made the bomb. They did so reluctantly. By then, they knew what had happened and also knew I wasn't going to let the debt go unpaid. Because now, I felt rage and I'm sure they could hear that in my voice. I wanted vengeance, pure and simple.

"Two of the three were brothers named Watson, something I found strange because it's a Scottish surname, not that it mattered to me. I didn't give a damn what their names were. The other's name was Conn Cleary, and he lived in a second floor walkup in Crumlin, a suburb of Dublin. One of my contacts provided that much. He didn't yet know where the Watsons lived, so Cleary came first.

"Handguns are not impossible to come by in Ireland, but are difficult, and frankly, I didn't want to connect with the criminal element to get one. A set of heavyweight steak knives would do nicely and that's what I bought at a second hand shop. There were six in the set and I only needed three so tossed three in a trash bin.

"Cleary was a drinker with a favorite pub, which was fine by me. Closing time was twelve-thirty with an additional half hour to drink up and he stayed till the last minute. I followed him to his flat twice, once giving him a light for his cigarette. The third time, I followed close behind him and went into the building with him before he could close the front door. In his drunken state, I think he mistook me for another border and I followed him up the flight of stairs to his room. When he opened his door, I shoved him in. He sprawled on the floor and I dragged him to a straight backed chair, sat him down and then slapped his face till he came round enough to understand me. I asked him if he remembered London. Remembered Marble Arch and the bomb. I told him that it was my sweetheart they'd murdered. He knew. He remembered. His eyes got wide and he started to say he didn't have anything to do with it, that it was Benny someone. That's when I slammed the knife into the center of his chest just under the breastbone. The shock took his breath and I worked the knife back and forth, slicing his heart to shreds. He lost consciousness and was dead in a couple minutes. I left the knife in him and took a small piece of paper out of my pocket that had one word printed on it: London. I laid it on his chest. I wanted the Watsons to know and I knew word would get out whether the police made it public or not. I was wearing gloves and had no worry about prints or any other identification. I had blood on the front of my jacket but simply took it off and folded it over my arm. Then I left, went back to my room, drank a stiff whiskey and went to bed.

"I caught up with one of the two Watsons about ten days later and finished him the same way but it was in an alley behind a metal shop. The other Watson brother fled to the Borders area near Northern Ireland and I decided not to follow. I knew I'd stick out like a sore thumb in the Borders but more than that, I simply wanted to return to the States. I came back, left my contract job and drank myself from one place to another till I met Ben Parker, our boss. He helped me get sober and stay that way. And then I met you, my special, special lady. Some people say everything happens for a reason. I don't know about that. I don't care about that. What I do know is you've become the love of my life and the light of my life."

Deirdre stood up, walked a couple steps to Hays and sat down on his lap, and wrapped both arms around his neck. She kissed him very lightly on the lips. "Never, ever in my life, will I love as deeply as I love you."

He nuzzled her neck. "I think it's a cuddle night. Tomorrow might be a long day and a busy one."

She agreed.

# Chapter 4

They didn't have any trouble finding the Village Inn and when directed to the booths along the windows, didn't have any trouble finding Jake either. There were only four people in the section, a rather old, diminutive cowboy with white beard, two women having pancakes and coffee, and a big Indian in the corner booth. Jake was medium dark, partly from ancestry and partly from working outdoors, with long black hair pulled back in a ponytail. His face was beginning to show the lines of someone in his mid forties and he was undoubtedly big. Jake rose as they came to the table and Hays judged him to be at least six-feet-three and a very hard 220 pounds.

They introduced themselves, shook hands and sat down. Jake looked at Dierdre and then to Hays before saying, "You're right."

Hays laughed. "For God's sake, no comments about outhouses. She threatened to raise my voice by three octaves last night."

Jake looked back at Dierdre. "I bet she could do it too." Hays suspected that left unsaid was,

"In more ways than one," but figured the less said the better.

They ordered coffee and breakfast for all three. Hays had decided that morning not to hold anything back from Jake, including the information that had about the gold mask. If Jake was going to guide them, he'd have to have access to Evan's notes and being selective about it didn't make sense.

"Adrian trusts you, so we will too. All we ask is if you decide you can't or won't guide us into the Jemez Mountains, that you don't say anything to anyone about us and what we're looking for. Fair enough?

"Yeah, fair enough, but I've already decided to guide you. I been settin' forms and pourin' concrete six days a week for nine weeks now and need a break. Some time in the mountains will give that to me. Now tell me about Begay and where we'll be headed."

Hays filled him in with everything he knew, starting with Anna Begay's phone call to him in Columbus. Their food arrived and Hays continued talking between bites, relating everything in chronological order including Evan's claim to have found a gold mask.

Jake hadn't said a word the whole time and when he finished eating, he sat back from the table, and waited while the server refilled their coffee cups. "I take it no one found the mask at his camp. Did they find any maps of where he might have been looking?"

Dierdre sat her coffee cup down and said, "We have maps of the area he was concentrating on, and of course where his camp was found when he disappeared. Also a lot of notes that we're still sorting through, but if he marked any maps with important locations just before he disappeared, we haven't seen them. Unless..." She turned to Hays. "Does Anna have the laptop he took with him?"

"Damn, I didn't think to ask. We'll call her when we get back to the room."

Jake looked out the window for a moment, thinking. "Depending on where he was, if he was on or near Redondo Peak, he may have been in a restricted area. Most of that land, including the Valles Caldera, belonged to the Baca family till they sold it to the government for a park. We'd be trespassing like he was if we go in there. And with the exception of a few sections, what doesn't belong to the government belongs to the Jemez Pueblo" He smiled. "Not that I haven't been there, understand. Some people have been known to poach deer on that land."

"Does that include you, Jake," asked Dierdre.

"No ma'am, sure doesn't."

"Don't like breaking the law?"

"No... Don't like venison. Won't pass on Elk, though."

Hays picked up his coffee. "We were thinking of renting a camping trailer this afternoon. Maybe head up that way in the morning. Can you be ready that soon?"

"I can be ready this afternoon. No need to rent a trailer, though. I have a two year old hard-side that sleeps six and a four wheel drive to pull it. If you can be ready about three o'clock, I can be at your hotel. It's about three hours to get to an area near Redondo, but outside the restricted area.

That'll give us enough time to set up camp before dark. You have any firearms?"

"We borrowed some of Evan's from Anna Begay. Couple of rifles, a shotgun, and two handguns. Three o'clock sounds fine. We should be able to pick up Evan's laptop by then if Anna has it. How about food and other supplies?"

"I'll pick up some things when I leave here but it will probably be sandwiches for tonight. That OK?"

"That's fine. Be sure to get receipts for groceries and other supplies. I'll reimburse you for them."

"One other thing: do you have broad brimmed hats to wear? If not, stop by one of the Western wear places and pick up a couple of straws. We'll be over 7000 feet in that area and the sun is a bear at that altitude."

"We'll get hats on the way back to the hotel, and by the way, were in room 215 if you have to call."

Jake stood up from the table, smiling. "Didn't think it was separate rooms for some reason. Alright. Can't think of anything else offhand. See you at three."

Hays took his cell phone from his shirt pocket and tapped in Anna's number. She answered on the second ring. "Hi Anna, it's Hays. We'll be heading up to the Jemez Mountains this afternoon. Ssomething I forgot to ask when we talked with you: Did the searchers find Evan's mini laptop at his camp?"

""No, they didn't. I specifically asked about it and was told they didn't find it at the camp. And I'm as forgetful as you. I meant to say something to you about it yesterday and forgot. I'm sorry."

"Nothing to be sorry for Anna. Hell, I forgot to ask. We have our guide. His name is Jake Nez and he talks like he's very familiar with the area. I'll give you a call tomorrow evening to let you know how we're doing. That OK?"

"That's fine, Hays. Listen... I don't know how to thank you. Just the fact that you and Dierdre are here..."

"No thanks needed, Anna. We'll call tomorrow." He turned to Dierdre. "No reason to go back to Anna's. No laptop. We'll stop at that Western Warehouse we passed on the way here and get some hats, then go back to the hotel and pack up. Shouldn't take long. Maybe even have time for a nap."

"You old fart! You've never taken a nap in your life. I know... you've had a big breakfast and just want me to rub your tummy."

He smiled. "Yeah, or something like that."

By the time they stopped at the western wear store, bought hats, and returned to the hotel, it was almost noon. Hays had picked out an off-white cowboy hat with rancher crease and Dierdre, a tan Australian outback style straw. They tried them on again after they were in their room.

"Starting to look the part," said Hays, "though I draw the line at cowboy boots. At least for what we're going to be doing and where."

Dierdre was looking at herself in the full-length mirror. "Jeans, denim shirt, outback hat – I think I could fit in to the Southwest easily. I do look pretty good."

"No modesty in your ancestry. But you do look good enough to eat."

"Is that an offer?"

"Well, we have time for a quick hitter."

"Boy, are you a romantic son of a bitch!"

They were both laughing. Dierdre took her hat off and posed, cocking one leg. "Hat on or hat off?"

"Everything off. You can use the hat to cover the nasty bits."

She put the hat back on her head and began to take of her clothes in a hasty version of a strip-tease beginning with blouse, bra, shoes, jeans and panties; one by one, each piece being tossed on the chair near the round occasional table. She then took off the hat and put it low on her stomach so that the chin-strap hung down between her legs with the brim barely covering her thick, curly auburn hair. Hays started to get up from the edge of the bed but she tossed her hat on the chair, stepped forward and pushed him back, saying, "I'm in charge this time, fella."

She pulled his shirt off over his head, then moved to loosen his belt, unzip his fly and pull his pants down around his ankles. She slipped off his loafers and socks, then his pants. Running both her hands up the inside of his legs, she slid them under the edge of his underpants and began to fondle gently, bringing an immediate reaction. His legs were still dangling over the edge of the bed and grasping the edge of his underpants, she pulled them down to his ankles, then off. She started kissing him at the inside of his left thigh just above the knee, slowly moving upward, and when her mouth closed on him it was as if the heat from her body flashed into him and crept rapidly up his abdomen.

"Jesus!"

She murmured something unintelligible as her tongue moved round and round and round... She released him and began to move upward slowly, planting soft kisses on his abdomen, stomach, chest, and finally his mouth. She straddled him, and with one hand, put him in her. Then, leaning back, sitting almost upright she began moving forward and backward, head thrown back, eyes closed, breathing hard. His hands, tight to her thighs, thumbs in the creases where her legs met, moved with her, pulling and pushing, his breathing as hard as hers, till the both reached orgasm and she slowly collapsed to his chest.

For perhaps three minutes, neither said anything, nor did they move. Then they both giggled. No reason, just happy.

Finally, he said, "I'm going to buy you a hat more often. God knows what you'd do if I bought you a baseball cap."

She kissed him on the ear. "Try it and see."

"Not today, honey, not today. Want to share a shower?"

"No, go ahead. I'll finish packing our things, but give me a holler when you're done."

# Chapter 5

Jake was ten minutes early but they were ready to go when he phoned from the lobby. The trailer was a beauty – large and sleek, of flat-brushed aluminum with rounded edges, and slightly more than twenty-five feet long. Not an Airstream but similar. It was hitched to a big Ford F-250 four door.

Before leaving and for fifty bucks, Hays arranged for their rental SUV to be returned to the airport.

He opened the forward-most of two side doors to the trailer. "Just toss your bags on the floor. They'll be fine till we get there and then I'll give you a guided tour."

They took I-25 north to the Bernalillo exit and then headed northwest on Route 550, a wide four lane that ran to Aztec and on into Colorado. About 40 minutes later, at San Ysidro, they turned off Route 550 onto Route 4 and headed in a more northerly direction.

Jake lit a Camel. "This is a smoke free truck

and what's behind us is a smoke free trailer. That means you can feel free to smoke in both."

Dierdre, who was in back and had stretched her legs out across the seat, smiled and said, "You have a strange way of putting things."

"I could be a wise guy and say it's a Navajo way of saying things, but its not. It's just my way. I pretty much smoke where I want unless someone has a serious objection."

Hays lit his pipe and took several puffs. "Serious objection?"

"Yeah, like a gun in my ribs."

They all laughed.

Dierdre leaned forward. "Speaking of Navajo, and I don't want to offend anyone, but do you prefer to be called a Native American, or Indian, or what?"

Jake looked at Hays. "She always come straight out with questions like that?"

"Always."

Jake looked at Dierdre in the rear view mirror. "Well now, where were you born?"

"In northern Ohio."

"Kinda makes you a Native American, doesn't it? Sure as hell doesn't make you a Native Russian."

"Yeah, but..."

"Native American is a politically correct label some yuppies on the east coast dreamed up. Makes them feel less guilty, I guess. Less guilty of what, though, I don't know. I'm an American Indian – or to be more precise, I'm Navajo. I'm not *a Navajo*, I'm Navajo, and there's a difference I won't go into right now. Most Indians identify themselves with their nation, such as Navajo, Zuni, Hopi, and so on. Apache, who are kin to the Navajo by the way, tend to identify with their tribe such as the White Mountain Apache in Arizona, or the Jicarilla and Mescalero tribes in New Mexico. But to an outsider, they might simply say Apache.

"A lot of Indians say they are Indian first before anything else, and I guess that's to be expected because they're such a minority. And a poor one at that, till the pueblos and reservations received court approval for gambling casinos. A lot are still poor. There's a lot of disease rampant in the Indian population – diabetes for one - and booze takes a terrible toll. My father died of alcoholism when I was sixteen and two years later I was in the Army. I was Airborne – paratroopers – and finished high school while I was in. I liked the Army and was a Sergeant when I got out. Had to get out, really. My mother was having a hard time, though she wouldn't say so. She died three years later. Now there's only me and my sister. But I guess I'd say I'm American first and Navajo second but that doesn't sit well with some people. ...And I haven't rattled on like this in years. Not like me to talk so much."

Deirdre rested her hand lightly on Jake's shoulder. "Well, I'm glad you did, Jake. Most of what I know about Indians comes from movies and newspapers and I've always had a feeling both were a lousy source."

"Yeah, mostly they are. Redford's made some movies that are decent and occasionally the local papers turn out an accurate piece, but for the most part they're really out of touch. And as far as novelists are concerned, Tony Hillerman probably wrote more accurately about the Navajo than any historian."

Hays had put his pipe in his shirt pocket and was looking at one of the maps Anna had given them. "We have the location of Begay's camp marked on this map but it looks like it may be in a restricted area or at least close. I don't think we can camp there."

"Never intended to. No sense stirring shit. I had a pretty good idea where his camp was from what you said at the restaurant, so we'll set up a bit less than two miles away on some land owned by a friend of mine. He's run electricity to a small clearing about a half mile from his house. I've camped there before. Nothing fancy but it's secluded and we won't be bothered."

They passed through the Jemez Indian Reservation, Jemez Springs, and then a few miles north of Jemez Springs, they turned left onto a hard packed gravel road. Jake lit a Camel and they traveled another half mile before the road split into a Y and he took the left branch. "We're traveling roughly parallel to the western boundary of the Baca land. The road that goes off to the right deadends there at a locked gate. We should be where we're going to camp in less than ten minutes."

Dierdre shifted in the back seat. "None too soon. The lady needs a pee break."

Jake put his Camel in a snuff-out container and turned his head slightly toward her. "It'll take a few minutes to set the trailer up. You might want to find a tall bush or a wide tree if you can't wait."

"No problem. I've been camping with that

barbarian in the front seat often enough. Bushes don't bother me."

Hays turned, grinning. "Barbarian? What the hell..."

Dierdre interrupted him, leaning forward toward Jake. "He thinks a Lady-J is civilized – tames the wilderness."

They were coming up on a small log house that sat one hundred feet or so off the road and Jake was slowing down. "Lady-J can come in handy though. Long time ago, the women of some tribes would hold pissing contests. I won't go into detail..."

Dierdre was laughing. "Oh, this I gotta hear."

"Nah, I don't know you well enough." Jake was smiling as he pulled to the side of the road just shy of a double gate that opened to a one-lane dirt track. "I'll tell Hays and he can pass it on."

Jake pulled over to the far side of the road about thirty feet short of the lane, stepped from the truck and swung both sections of the gate inward, giving them an opening twenty feet wide. As he got back in, he said, "Fellow who owns this land isn't here right now but I expect he'll visit us later for a cup of coffee. Name's Leantree, John Leantree. Born on the Jemez Pueblo. Most folks call him Bark, and before you ask, I don't know if it's the bark of a dog, bark of a tree, or something else. Never asked him. But he's a wise old man and one helluva tracker. Taught me a lot, anyway."

Hays got out of the truck. "You go ahead and pull through. I'll watch the trailer and close the gate."

The pickup and trailer pulled ahead, then

across the road and through the gate with a smooth, practiced motion that cleared the opening with room to spare. Hays closed and fastened the gate and got back in the truck, pulling his pipe from his pocket as he settled back in the seat. He tamped, lit, and took a few puffs. "You say Mr. Leantree is a tracker, Jake. Will he be offering to help?"

"I doubt it. He's pretty busy this time of year. He installs and repairs air conditioners – out here we call them swamp coolers – and does some small construction jobs. He might help if asked but only if he's free. We'll look around a bit first and decide if we need him."

Less than five minutes down the lane brought them to a small, oblong meadow surrounded on three sides by fir and aspen trees. Jake drove to the far end, wheeled in a half circle that put the trailer about twenty feet from the tree line and stopped. "OK, folks, we're home." He turned to Dierdre who was opening the back door. "Watch for snakes."

"If they're close, they're going to get wet." She disappeared into the trees.

Forty minutes later, they were sitting in comfortable camp chairs, sipping coffee and watching the sun slide behind the tree line of a mountain several miles away. Hays lit his pipe and turned to Jake. "What sort of wildlife is found here?"

"Quite a mix. Just about everything but brown bear, mountain lion, and wolves, and I'm not sure about mountain lion. The only wolves in New Mexico are the Mexican Grays reintroduced down southwest of Dillon, and this just isn't brown bear country. I've heard tell of mountain lion but in all my time here, have never seen track. But there's black bear, deer, elk, lynx, coyote, and a bunch of other smaller critters. The only one of concern is black bear. Females might have cubs this time of year and they're unpredictable as hell. If you spot one before they see you, steer clear. If you come face to face with one, back away slowly. Whatever you do, don't run. When you run, the bear goes into prey mode and will chase you. Unless you climb a tree damned quick, they can outrun you anyway. They can climb trees too but they generally won't bother. If they act aggressively, raise your arms and holler loud. If you appear bigger to them than they are, sometimes they'll go away.

"And if they don't?" asked Dierdre.

"Shoot 'em. Not legal of course, but I'd rather take my chances explaining my actions to a judge than to my Maker." Jake started to say something else, paused, and frowning, turned his head toward the far end of the clearing. Standing, he looked at Hays for a few seconds, then turned to go into the trailer. "Keep talking. I'll be back in a minute."

Less than a minute later, he was back carrying the coffee pot in his left hand and carton of half & half in his right. "Anyone want a refill?"

Hays set his pipe on the small table next to his chair and reached for his cup. "Yeah, I think I do." Then, in a low voice, "Did you see something we should know about?"

"Heard. Two men I think, moving around the

clearing from the far end about thirty feet back in the trees."

"How can you tell?"

"I'd like to say it's an Indian thing, but one of them must have stumbled because I heard him say, 'ah shit,' and another voice saying something but I couldn't make it out. When I went into the trailer, I stuck a .45 auto in the back of my jeans. Ya never know."

For several minutes, they sat drinking coffee and talking before two men emerged from the tree line about fifty feet away and came toward the trailer. Both appeared to be in their mid thirties and the same height; about six feet. The one slightly to the front had dark brown hair, neatly trimmed beard, and walked with the easy gait of one used to being outdoors and walking long distances. The second man was fair, blonde, clean-shaven, muscular, and shuffled his feet slightly. Hays assumed he was the one who stumbled. The bearded one spoke first.

"Evening. Doing a bit of camping?" He spoke to Jake but his eyes undressed Dierdre who had taken the coffee pot and was standing next to Hays, pouring a cup.

"Yeah, a bit," answered Jake, shifting slightly to his left in the chair. "You fellas camping or you live around here?"

"Nah, we live in Albuquerque but come up here all the time. Mostly tent camping. Milt here," he nodded toward the blonde, "has a soft-side trailer but we move around so much a tent is easier. If we're going to fish Fenton or the Jemez River, we'll use the trailer but mostly it's the tent. My name's Stevens, by the way, Bill Stevens, and this is Milt

Chambers." Jake introduced himself, Hayes, and Dierdre.

Stevens was looking at the trailer. "That's a helluva nice rig you have. Looks big enough to be a home away from home. Planning to be here long?"

Jake stood and placed his cup on the table. "Maybe five days. Not sure. But you're right about the camper. I've lived in it for a month or more during hunting season."

Hays made a decision based purely on intuition. "Actually, we're looking for someone; a Navajo named Evan Begay who disappeared up here several weeks ago." If he was looking for reaction, he got it. Not from Stevens, but from Chambers who had been looking at Jake's truck. His head snapped around and he looked first at Hays and then to Stevens, but didn't say anything.

It was Stevens who spoke. "Yeah, we heard about that. In fact, we were in Jemez Springs when the Sheriff came through with a search and rescue team. Had dogs too, as I remember. They didn't find him, huh?"

"No, not a trace – other than his camp, that is. They called the search off after a week but his wife doesn't want to give up. We promised her we'd spend a few days looking around. Maybe pick up on something the search team missed."

"Well, I wish you luck but I doubt you'll find him. Those rescue teams are pretty thorough. We'd better head back to our camp and fix something to eat. Gettin' late." Stevens took a step back and nodded to Chambers indicating it was time to go.

They watched them walk the length of the

meadow before disappearing into the woods. Hays turned toward Jake. "What do you think?"

"Not sure. I thought Chambers' head was going to corkscrew off his shoulders when you said we were looking for Begay, but it might not mean anything."

"You don't believe that."

Jake smiled. "No, I don't believe that."

"They got out of here in a hurry, too," said Dierdre.

Jake took the .45 from his belt and set it on the table. "Yeah, they did, and I bet they've already eaten. I doubt we'll have any trouble tonight but beginning tomorrow morning, we'd better keep a lookout for those two."

Hays turned toward the table, picked up his pipe and was lighting it when he was startled by a voice that came from out of sight at the back end of the trailer.

"I seen them two fellows up here before."

Jake turned toward the voice. "That you, Leantree?"

"Yeah... You hear me comin' up the path?"

"Nope, we're downwind. I smelled you. Musta had refried beans with lunch."

"Damn!" From around the back of the trailer came an Indian, perhaps sixty, but could have been older. He was short, maybe five feet-eight and whipcord lean. His face was dark, angular, and etched with lines from years of living and working outdoors in the sun. His hair, once black but now streaked with lines of gray, was long and pulled back in a ponytail that hung down his back from under a battered, black, wide-brimmed hat. He wore desert boots and a muted red-brown patterned shirt tucked into Wrangler jeans that must have been blue once, but only hinted at that color now.

He walked up to the camp table, glancing at Hays and Dierdre. "You must have just come in here today, Jake. You guiding tourists now?"

Jake smiled. "In a manner of speaking. You want some coffee?"

"Sure, and a chair. My ass is draggin'. Replaced two coolers today and didn't finish up till about three o'clock. And you're right about the beans. Tamales too."

Jake went into the trailer and returned a minute later with a cup and another folding chair. He nodded toward Hays and Dierdre. "This is Hays McKay and Dierdre Stuart. Folks, this is John Leantree but he answers to Bark." Leantree made no move to shake hands but he nodded.

"They've asked me to do some guiding for them," continued Jake. "They're looking for Evan Begay, or his remains, which is more likely."

Leantree cocked his head slightly and squinted at them. "Yeah, likely. You kin?"

"No," said Hays, pausing to relight his pipe. "We're friends of Anna Begay, Evan's wife."

Leantree lifted his cup and took a sip. "Damn good coffee. What is it?"

"Kenya Estate," said Jake. "Got it at Moon's on Juan Tabo. She roasts fresh every day. Got any idea where we might start looking for Begay?"

"When was the last anybody heard from him?"

"Saturday evening, the day before he was to come home, he called his wife. That's the last time anyone heard from him that we know of," said

Hays as he tapped the ash out of his pipe, refilled it and put a match to the bowl.

"Then he was probably in camp or not far from it – say a mile or so."

"The search party covered the entire area."

Leantree was quiet for a moment, then took a sip of coffee. "Maybe they did and maybe they didn't."

"What do you mean?"

"There are areas on the mesas and mountain you can walk past game or a man at ten feet and not see 'em." Leantree stood up. "Thanks for the coffee, Jake."

"You're welcome, Bark. Any suggestions?"

"Follow the trickster's trail." Leantree nodded to Hays and Dierdre and walked back toward his cabin.

"Who's the trickster?" asked Dierdre as she reached out, took the pipe from Hays' hand, puffed twice, and then handed it back.

Jake had an astonished look on his face. "She do that often?"

"Only when she's trying to get attention," said Hays, smiling. "Who is the trickster?"

"What, actually. Coyote. Commonly called the trickster and sometimes jokester. They're one of the smartest animals on four legs and smarter than most with two. Seem to be able to survive anywhere, whether in and around cities or in the wild. They scavenge a lot and won't pass up a free meal. If Begay is dead and his body's well hidden, the coyote would still find him by scent. That's what Leantree meant. Look for heavy coyote track where maybe there shouldn't be."

"Makes sense," said Hays.

Dierdre stood, picked up the empty coffee pot and headed into the trailer. "What time do we start tomorrow?"

Jake was folding the camp chairs and leaning them against the table. "Early... just after sunup. We have about a forty-five minute walk from here. Come on, I'll show you how the shower works. It's a bit tricky."

# Chapter 6

Hays was awake, lying on his back staring at the light beginning to creep through the window when there was a tap at the door. "Drop your whatever and grab your socks, it's a little after five. Coffee's on."

"Thanks, Jake. I can smell it." He turned to Dierdre who was awake and looking out the window as he had been.

"Sure gets bright in a hurry here, doesn't it?"

Hays had slipped on a pair of jeans and was reaching for a pipe. "Well, New Mexico is known for it's sunshine and at this altitude it's probably even more noticeable. Want me to bring you a cup of coffee?"

"I'd love it. I'll hit the shower while you're getting the go-juice."

Hays filled his pipe, a large old Charatan bent, lit it and walked to the front of the trailer. Jake was sitting at the table sipping coffee and smoking a cigarette.

"Jake, you're going to have to upgrade – you need two bathrooms."

"If you have to pee, the other one's outside and around the back."

"Sparkling idea," said Hays, resting his pipe against a large ashtray. "I'll be right back. Pour me a cup, would you. Just black."

He was back in a couple of minutes, sat down at the table, took a sip of coffee and then relit his pipe. "Are all the mornings like this?" asked Hays. "Its crisp and clear and there's a soft scent of wild flowers in the air."

Jake set his cup on the table. "Almost always, at least in the mountains away from the cities. We have over three hundred days of sunshine a year but summer temperatures aren't as oppressive as some places in Arizona like Tucson, Phoenix, and points south. Las Cruses gets hot but the middle and northern part of the state has moderate temperatures. Albuquerque only had two days of hundred degree temps last year.

"The mountains are what I love, but believe me, it snows up here in wintertime. Not unusual to have two feet or more on the ground with roads drifted over. Folks that live in the mountains stock up on basics in the fall and try to keep a ten day supply on hand. And people in small communities like Jemez Springs look out for each other and check on neighbors regularly. Cell phones have made things easier but service is still spotty in some areas. It's a nice place to be for now."

"It certainly is that, Jake. How far is it to where Evan had his camp?"

Jake stubbed his cigarette out in the ashtray. "Not far, but in any case, we'll walk. I think we're going to be in a restricted area and I don't want the truck nearby. I figure it'll take about forty

79

minutes to get there, maybe a bit more. We should find signs of his camp, though I expect the sheriff's cleared out all his gear."

"Other than maps, is there anything special we should take with us?

"Handguns, I guess. I'll carry a .38 revolver loaded with birdshot in case of rattlers and take along a daypack with some bottled water and munchies too. Hard to tell how long we'll be but I expect we'll miss lunch." He turned toward the rear of the trailer. "Your gal is out of the shower. I'll get the pack ready, so you go next and I'll follow. I'd like to be out of here in a half hour or so."

A forty minute uphill walk, first through a forest of fir and cedar, then scrub, brought them to a wide, barren mesa strewn with a few huge boulders and smaller outcroppings of volcanic rock. Off to their left, the plateau continued to rise slightly till it butted up against a mountain that rose sharply against the azure blue sky. They walked to the edge of the mesa and could see far off in the distance, a small town.

"That's Jemez Springs," said Jake, "and the small line of smoke you see rising off in the distance is probably from San Ysidro, thirty miles away.

Deirdre glanced over the edge of the mesa and then backed away a few steps. "And how far down is it?"

"About 600 feet... a bit less as the land below rises toward the mountain."

Hays was looking at the map. "I think we're close to where Begay was camped. Let's spread out and see if we can find some sign of it. Maybe form a line and work toward the mountain first."

They had walked about 200 feet when Deirdre shouted, "Over here!"

As they approached, she continued, "Looks like signs of a camp. There's still a screw-in tent peg in the ground the sheriff must have missed and I'm guessing, but under that flat wide rock about 20 feet off, we might find a latrine.

Jake walked over to the rock and using a stout stick lying next to it, flipped the rock upright so that it was propped against another nearby. "She's right. It's about two feet deep and he burned his paper." He poked around with the stick. "Nothing else..."

Hays was facing Jake, lighting his pipe, when his left leg went out from under him. He knew what it was before he heard the echoing sound of the shot and hollered, "Gun!" as he was falling. Deirdre threw herself into a slight depression a few feet away and Jake hit the ground behind the latrine rock that afforded little cover but was better than nothing. Hays lay still, not moving. Perhaps two minutes went by before he asked, "See anything?"

Jake turned his head slightly toward Hays. "Not a thing. No movement anywhere."

Deirdre had crawled to the south end of the depression. "I think the shot came from that outcropping of trees about 200 yards away. It's a short distance from where we came up to the top of the mesa."

Hays rolled over onto his back. "Going to have to take a chance, folks, I'm bleeding like hell."

Deirdre was next to him in an instant, kneeling

at his waist and reaching for a handkerchief in her back pocket.

Hays half rose. "Get down, dammit!"

"No!" She pulled a Spyderco knife from her belt, thumbed it open, sliced across his pantleg from the bullet hole, and laid the top of the opening back. The wound was ten inches above his knee in the meaty part of his thigh with entrance and exit about three inches apart. The entrance wound toward the back of his leg was simply a puncture but the bullet had torn a piece of flesh loose the size of a quarter on exit. She put the flap of skin back in place, then pressed a folded handkerchief over it and in a voice that brooked no argument, told Hays to put his hand on top and apply pressure. She turned toward Jake. "You got a first aid kit in that pack?"

Jake rolled once away from the rock, stood, then walked over to them. "May as well get shot as lay downwind of that latrine." He laid the pack on the ground, took out a couple bottles of water and a field first aid kit. "Let's see what we've got."

Hays raised up on one elbow and lifted the handkerchief. Blood immediately began to seep from the wound. Jake opened one of the bottles of water and looked at Hays. "We'll flush it, then wrap it. Doesn't look to be deep enough to have nicked an artery or you'd be squirting all over the place. The real problem is going to be getting you out of here. You need a doctor and stitches. I could call for a rescue chopper on my cell..."

"No... if you wrap it tight and give me a hand, I think I can make it back to the truck. We don't want to invite more trouble than what we have and bringing in the authorities would do just that."

Jake glanced at Deirdre and she nodded her head in agreement. He tore away the rest of the pantleg, flushed the wound with water and wrapped it before helping Hays to his feet, then stepped back leaving him unsupported. "Can you walk?"

Hays took a couple of steps. "Hurts, but I can walk slowly. I'll probably need help when we hit that steep incline."

Jake took his cell phone from his pocket and flipped the lid up. "Let me see where Leantree is." He tapped in a number with his thumb, then listened for a few seconds. "Leantree? Jake... Your Jeep running? Good. One of my friends has been shot... No, not bad - in the leg. Can you make it to the base of the mesa northeast of my camp? OK... About thirty minutes or so. Thanks."

"Leantree will meet us at the bottom of the slope and save us more than a mile's walk to our camp. When we get to that steep incline, it's probably best you go down backwards - less strain on the leg. You can hang onto Deirdre and me. We'll take my truck into the urgent care clinic in Rio Rancho. I don't think they have a triage unit but it probably doesn't matter because the bullet went through. Cleaned up and stitched should do it."

Hays was staring at the ground where he had fallen. "Bastard!" He took two limping steps. "Bastard!"

Deirdre moved next to him. "You said that once."

Hays was still looking at the ground. "When I fell, it broke the stem of my pipe. Damn fine

83

Charatan, too. The bastard! Would you get it for me, honey?"

She walked a few feet, bent, picked up the two pieces of pipe and gave them to Hays. "Can it be repaired?

"I think so. It broke at the tenon where it goes into the shank. I'm going to get that bastard. Oughta take the pipe and shove it up his ass bowl first."

Jake picked up the first aid kit, put it in the pack and slipped it onto his shoulder. "Hang onto that thought - should make getting to Leantree easier."

Leantree was waiting for them when they got to the base of the hill. They helped Hays into the front seat of an old open Jeep and Jake took a look at his leg. "Not bleeding much, Hays. I'm surprised. Thought sure it would open up coming down the hill." He turned to Leantree. "Just get us back to our camp. I'll take him into RR to have him patched up."

Leantree slid behind the wheel while Deirdre and Jake got into the back seat. As they started out, Leantree glanced at Hays. "I take it that wasn't self inflicted."

Hays shifted slightly, trying to keep his leg straight. "Not hardly."

They switched to Jake's truck at their camp. Hays tried to convince Deirdre to stay at the camp but was met with a firm refusal and felt too miserable to argue the point. At the clinic, Jake did the talking, saying they were just north of Jemez Springs enjoying a walk along the river when Hays was shot. They figured it was someone hunting prairie dogs some distance off because they barely heard the sound of the shot and didn't see anyone. In any case, they were more interested in getting medical attention for Hays than to spend time looking around. After stitches, a tetanus shot and another to dull the pain, a Deputy Sheriff, called by the clinic, walked in and they had to explain again what happened, this time in writing. When they returned to their camp, Leantree was still there.

"You had visitors but I didn't see anyone. Felt 'em first, then heard 'em. I think they was debating coming in, but I leisurely wandered over to my Jeep and fussed in the back like I was looking for a gun or something Spect it might have discouraged 'em. I fixed a pot of coffee a few minutes ago. Would've fixed something to eat too, but figured it was a might early. How's the leg?"

Hays limped over to a camp chair and sat down. "If I were a drinking man, I'd have a drink but I'll settle for coffee. It's not all that bad, really. They gave me a shot at the clinic and some pills for later. I'll be sore but alright."

Leantree handed him a cup of coffee. "You think it was intentional?"

"We talked about that on the way back. Yeah, I think it was intentional. I'm not sure whoever it was intended to hit me, but shooting in our direction was intentional. We were out in the open and the shot came from the edge of some trees about 200 yards off. He couldn't mistake who he was shooting at and I suspect they were just trying to scare us, but I have a gut feeling it was Stevens and Chambers, the two visitors we had yesterday. No way to prove it, though.

Deirdre sat down next to Hays and turned to Jake. "Can I bum a cigarette, Jake?"

"Sure - hell, I didn't know you smoked."

"I don't."

Hays grinned as Jake handed over a pack of Camels and lighter. "She smokes a couple a month whether she needs them or not."

Deirdre lit the cigarette, inhaled shallowly, and handed the pack to Jake, but held onto the lighter looking at it. It was an old worn Zippo but she could still make out the initials on the side: AB/JN.

Jake was watching her and as she handed the lighter to him, he said, "It was a gift from Adrian years ago. Zippos seem to last forever. Never got around to buying another."

Hays set his cup on the camp table. "Honey, would you get my pipe bag for me? I think its on the shelf by the bed." As she got up, he turned slightly toward Jake. "Adrian told me you two were close. I got the impression she was in love with you and maybe still is, but your worlds were too far apart to make a go of it."

"She must have told you a little more than you let on when we first talked."

"Not much, really, but it wasn't hard to figure out. She's a remarkable woman, Jake - make a helluva fine partner for any man."

Jake lit a cigarette, looked at the inscription on the lighter, and then put it in his pocket. "I guess I know that as well as anyone, but at the time we each had plans for our lives that just wouldn't mesh. Actually, she had plans and I was just kinda drifting. She wanted to settle back east somewhere and I just couldn't do that. I don't know exactly how to put it into words but my whole life is here - here in this high desert country. It's kinda like the land and me - well, we're part of each other. Here, I'm home - here I belong. Anywhere else, I'd always be a visitor. That make sense?"

"More than you know, Jake, more than you know."

Deirdre came out of the trailer and handed a small leather bag to Hays. "You fellas solve all our problems while I was gone?"

Hays took a straight Dunhill sandblast from the bag and began to fill it with tobacco. "Not really. We were just talking about Adrian..." Hays paused while he lit his pipe. "Jake was saying he wouldn't be comfortable living anywhere else than the southwest and I guess I understand that." Hays turned slightly and looked over his shoulder. "What happened to Leantree? The man's like a ghost."

Jake stubbed his cigarette out. "Gone home, I reckon, or out scouting the woods. Maybe looking for whoever he heard earlier. Hard to tell. He's been like that as long as I've know him and ghost is a good way to put it. You'll be talking to him, turn your back and he's gone without a sound. The surprising thing is that he often appears the same way - just like he materializes out of nothing."

Deirdre's cigarette had been laying in the ashtray and she put it out. "Is that an Indian thing?"

Jake laughed. "Hell no. You can hear me coming a mile off. It's just Leantree."

Hays tapped the the remaining tobacco from

his pipe into his hand and dumped it in the ashtray. "I think I'm going to call it a day, folks... Turn in early. I doubt I'll be up to going to the mesa tomorrow, or anywhere much farther than this table. I don't want to let up on the search though. Why don't the two of you plan to pick up where we left off? At the very least, you can eliminate some of the places we may have looked at today if we'd had the chance. I may be well enough after a day of hobbling around here to help out the day after."

"Not the day after," said Deirdre, smiling. "You have to go back into the clinic to have your wound checked and dressing changed."

Hays paused at the door of the trailer. "Well, if we go early enough, I might be able to spend some time up there... a few hours anyway. I have a feeling we're missing something the same way the Sheriff did. If it was an accident, then Evan should have been found. If it wasn't an accident, and I believe it wasn't, then the body has been disposed of or hidden. I'm convinced he's dead, and probably murdered for something he discovered. No proof, of course... just an educated guess." With that, he went into the trailer followed by Deirdre while Jake folded the camp chairs and leaned them against the hitch.

# Chapter 7

The following morning, soon after breakfast and without Hays, Deirdre and Jake arrived atop the mesa in approximately the same location where McKay was shot. They stood near the edge looking in both directions.

Deirdre shrugged. "There's nothing here. You'd think if Hays was hit by a warning shot, there'd be something obvious we were being warned against. I don't see anything."

"I don't either. Jake moved back about ten yards from the edge and stooped down. "Then again..."

"Find something?"

"Maybe... Leantree said to follow the trickster. There's coyote tracks here, wandering back and forth a bit as they usually do but generally moving north along the ridge. Looks like five in this pack. Let's follow and see where they lead."

They climbed the gradually sloping mesa uphill, skirting or jumping over several narrow crevasses, following tracks that wandered as far as thirty yards from the edge to within two or three feet. Just before they reached that part of the mesa that inclined sharply uphill they came to a crevasse deeper and wider than the others that ran diagonally away from the rim and uphill. At a point farthest away from the rim, Jake squatted again, examined the area near the edge and then stood.

"There's been more than one pack investigate this cut in the mesa; a larger pack from the looks of the tracks and more than once."

They both moved to the edge of the crevasse and looked down. It was about four feet wide at the point where they were standing and a little more than thirty feet long. It was deep, though, and they could see only twenty feet into it. The rest was lost in shadow.

Jake dropped his pack. "We might be able to see more when the sun is directly overhead but in the meantime..." He opened one of the pack's side pockets, pulled out an LED flashlight, walked to the edge and focused the beam at one end of the cut, working it slowly towards them.

"Over here, Deirdre... Look straight down. There's a ledge of sorts about 30 feet down with what looks like an arm hanging out into space."

"Yeah... It's an arm."

Jake moved back from the edge. "I've got some rope in the pack. I'll go down and take a look."

"No, you won't. I'll go down and take a look."

"Could be messy."

"You should see Hays' den if you want to see messy."

"He leave bodies laying around?"

"Everything else but. It's this simple. If you go

down and get into trouble, I can't haul you up. On the other hand..."

"Yeah - see what you mean.

Jake drove two pitons into the rock, three feet apart and twenty feet from the edge, attached D-rings and threaded the rope through them that he took from his pack. He handed her the flashlight. "We have about 100 feet of 5/8 polypropylene rope here, which is more than enough. Better not touch anything... just confirm it's a body and maybe Begay if you can get a look at the face."

Deirdre formed two loops with the rope, stepped into them and then tied a loop around her waist as Jake watched.

"You done this before?"

"I've done some climbing and have used a harness but not a makeshift one like this. Just seems like a good idea."

Jake wrapped the rope around his waist and took a up the slack as she moved to the edge, turned, and leaned back before stepping downward.

"Just keep tension on it and I'll take rope as I need it."

"OK, boss, whatever you say." Standing about ten feet from the edge, he couldn't see her but judged her progress by the amount of rope played out. Finally, it stopped.

"What do you see?"

"Wait..." A half minute passed. "A body... Indian, I think... Shot in the leg. There's a small notebook... OK, help me up out of here."

Deirdre worked up the rope hand over hand as Jake backed away from the edge. She was up and out in less than a minute, and dropped the rope on the ground. There was a small notebook tucked in her belt.

"We'll have to get back to our camp and report this but I have a feeling we'd like to see what's in this notebook before the sheriff gets his hands on it. Anna Begay might eventually get it, but by then, we'd be back in Ohio and I think Hays would like to see it first."

As Jake made up the rope, Deirdre took out her cell phone and punched in Hays' number. He answered on the third ring. The connection was bad with a lot of static. "Mac, I think we've found Evan Begay."

"Hi Honey... You're breaking up. You say you've found Evan? Where?"

"On a ledge about 30 feet down in a crevasse. He'd been shot in the leg. I didn't disturb anything but there was a small notebook next to his right hand so I took it. Haven't even looked to see what was in it but thought we'd better go through it before we turn it over to the sheriff."

"Good thinking, but..."

"But?"

"But we'll have a hard time explaining why you took it in the first place and then held it for a while before turning it over."

"Maybe we don't have to turn it over. Maybe just give it to Anna."

"Maybe you're starting to think like me."

"Considering the connection, it's entirely likely."

"Speaking of connections..."

"Oh no! I know where your mind is going with that one and don't forget you've got a bum leg."

"I could hang it over the side..." Hays was

laughing. "What I was going to say before I was so crudely interrupted, was there may be something in the notebook that would make a connection between Evan being shot and whoever it is that wants us to clear out. How long will it be before you're back here?"

Deirdre looked around at Jake and saw he was ready to go. "We're leaving now. Probably 45 minutes."

"OK, see you then. Oh, by the way, we have a visitor. She's nice looking too..."

"What's in that medicine you're taking?"

"Seriously... It's Jake's sister, Jeanette. See ya when ya get here."

Deirdre turned to Jake. "Your sister's in camp."

"I meant to say something and forgot. I called her last night and asked if she could get a few days off. She's a helluva cook and loves this country as much as I do. Figured she could help out a bit if we're going to be gone from camp most of the time. Also don't know how long Hays will be laid up. In any case, she jumped at the chance and Leantree said he'd pick her up, but I didn't think she'd be here till evening."

"Before we leave," said Deirdre, "I want to take a few minutes and walk along that treeline where we think the shot came from that hit Hays. Maybe find something."

They'd walked about fifty yards, Deirdre along the edge of the scrub and trees and Jake about five paces in, when Jake said, "Got something." He bent, picked up something small and then came to Deirdre holding it in his hand. "25-06

93

cartridge case. Good round for Elk or any long range shooting."

"Put it in your pocket," said Deidre. "Hays will want to see it."

Hays was sitting in a camp chair in front of a small table lighting a pipe as Jake and Deirdre came into the clearing. He took a couple of puffs, tamped the tobacco down and relit. "Ah... the happy wanderers. Where's the notebook?"

Deirdre set her pack down. "Trade. Where's the coffee?"

A voice from inside the trailer said, "On the way."

Jeanette appeared in the doorway carrying three stacked cups in one hand and a coffee pot in the other. "Figured you'd want some by the time you got here. There's pan biscuits on the stove. Be ready in a couple of minutes."

Hays set his pipe in an ashtray. "I gotta tell ya, Jake, I could get used to this. Your sister is nurse, cook, and historian all in one. She's been telling me about the various legends and theories of why and how the Anasazi disappeared. Some I'd never heard before. She claims most of the theories are wrong, particularly the one about a lengthy drought being the cause."

Jake picked up three folding chairs that were leaning against the trailer, opened them up, and sat in one of them. "I don't put much stock in most of the theories either and doubt if any will ever be proven." He smiled, "Seems drought is just as likely as ET and flying saucers."

"That's what your sister says." Hays turned to Deirdre. "Notebook?"

She handed him the small notebook. "I haven't even looked…"

He turned it over, looking at the back and then the front. "Stained. Blood from the looks of it."

Laying it face down on the table, he opened the back cover and began turning pages one at a time from the back to the front.

Deirdre, smiling, winked at Jake. "He always does that. Looks at the ending to decide whether the whole book is worth a read." Turning to Hays, she asked, "Are we going to call the sheriff?"

Picking up his pipe, he relit and took a few puffs. "Yeah, in ten minutes or so. I think we need to take a look at Evan's last few entries. It's definitely Evan's. There's an address label on the back inside cover."

Jeanette came out of the trailer carrying a plate of biscuits, put them on the table, poured herself a cup of coffee, and sat in the remaining empty chair.

Hays found the last entry and began turning pages, looking over each one quickly and then going to the next. After a half dozen pages, he left the notebook open, turned it around and laid it on the table in front of the others. "The last three pages appear to be entries made after he was shot and lay dying in the crevasse. They ramble but will be helpful. I think it's the earlier entries that will tell us what we want to know. Jake, why don't you place the call to the sheriff? You're local and that might work out better than if Deirdre or I phoned."

Jake took a pack of Camels from his pocket, flipped one out and lit it. He then slipped a finger inside the cellophane and pulled out a slip of paper. In response to Hays' quizzical expression, he said, "Phonebook."

He unfolded the paper, found the number he was looking for, took out his cell phone and made the call.

"Hello, this is Jake Nez. I'd like to speak with the sheriff..."

"Well, interrupt him and tell him we found a body and think it's Evan Begay. I expect he'll come to the phone..."

"Sheriff? ...Right... Jake Nez. We found a body in a rock fissure that we believe to be Evan Begay. ...No, we haven't touched anything. We came back to our camp to make the call to you. You'll need a rescue team - he's about 30 feet down." Jake proceeded to give directions to their camp and told the sheriff they'd lead him and his crew to the body.

He stubbed out his cigarette in the ashtray. "The sheriff said he'd be here within an hour and the team will follow. I think we'd better tell him Deirdre went down to take a look just to be sure it was a body. There'll probably be signs of that anyway."

"No need to mention the notebook, though," said Hays, turning to Deirdre. "Honey, why don't you put it under our mattress for the time being? Actually, anywhere out of sight is good. We'll go over it this evening after the sheriff is gone. In the meantime, should we call Anna, or wait?"

"Wait," replied Deirdre immediately. "We believe it's Evan, everything points to it, but I think it would be better to wait till the sheriff confirms it. All we have is the notebook. The sheriff should find a wallet or some ID. If we call Anna, the sheriff is bound to find out somehow and want to know how we knew for sure."

Hays winked at Jake. "See? Quick thinker. That's why I like having her around."

Jake smiled. "That the only reason?"

"Alright boys, that's enough," said Deirdre picking up the notebook. "One other thing - if Jeanette knows Anasazi history like you say, she could be a lot of help."

Hays picked up his pipe and tamped down the ash. "I agree, but its up to her. What do you say, Jeanette, want to play detective? I should caution you, though... there might be some danger. I've already been shot, Evan's been murdered, and we're not sure who or how many are involved. Could get even nastier than it is."

Jake started to say something but Jeanette stood up and interrupted him. "You don't know how much I was hoping you'd ask. I was afraid you'd tell me to go home. I'll be glad to help in any way I can."

Hays looked at Jake. "Problem?"

"No... No, I guess not. Jeanette's about as stubborn as your partner. Wouldn't do me any good to object."

"OK, that settles it. We'll examine the notebook after dinner tonight. The sheriff should be gone by then and we should be able to take our time. I can also call Anna, something I'm not looking forward to."

Deirdre had come back outside. "I can call her if you like."

"Thanks honey, I thought about it but I think I should talk to her. It's me she knows and me she called in Ohio. Better I do it, but later - after its official."

"Oh, before I forget," said Jake, "we found a present for you." He reached in his pocket and gave Hays the shell casing.

Hays took it and turned it over in his hand. "A 25-06. Yeah, that would do it. Where'd you find it?"

"Right about where it should have been for someone to take a clear shot at you. It was about fifteen feet inside the treeline. I figure whoever took the shot, jacked another round into the chamber and lost sight of the empty casing, but didn't follow up with another shot for some reason."

"Well, I'm not going to thank the bastard for that."

"I wouldn't, either."

The sheriff arrived about 45 minutes later followed by a four man rescue team a half hour behind him. Jake and Deirdre led them to the mesa and two hours later they all returned to camp, two of the team carrying a sagging body bag that they loaded in the back of their SUV. As they did, the sheriff walked over to the table where Hays was sitting and put out his hand. "Al Kaplin, county sheriff."

Hays shook hands. "Pardon if I don't get up. Bum leg."

"So you're the one. Heard about it. Think it was a hunter?"

"Or someone taking target practice a ways off. We didn't see anyone."

"Just up here camping?"

"Partly. Have a seat." Hays lit his pipe. "We're

friends of Anna Begay. Actually, I'm the friend of Anna's. I knew her years ago in Ohio. She contacted me a week ago and asked for help looking for her husband..." He then explained at some length why they were in the Jemez Mountain area and that they had no intention of treading on the toes of the Sheriff's Department; that it had simply been luck that led them to the body.

The sheriff took a sip of water from a bottle he was carrying. "It's definitely Begay. I have his wallet. Not robbery. Money and credit cards still in it. He was shot in his right leg above the knee. Probably an accident, either self inflicted or a hunter. Either way, he must have been standing at the opening of the fissure and toppled in, landing on the ledge. What I don't understand is why we didn't find him, or at least why the dogs didn't find him."

Hays picked up his coffee and took a sip. "Could be you were either too early or too late. If he followed that route regularly, the dogs would pick up his scent all along the ridge. If he was still alive but unconscious, you'd have never known. If he wcre dead, it would have been several days before the odor would be noticeable to dogs along the rim and you'd probably already gone, or at least were searching another area. The coyotes picked up on it, but he'd most likely been dead a week by then." Hays lifted the coffee pot. "Would you like a cup?"

"Thanks, but I'd better pass. Paperwork, and I'll have to notify Mrs. Begay unless you want to talk to her first."

"I thought about it but I think its best that

it officially come from you. You can tell her you talked with me and I'll call her later."

"You going to be headed back home now?"

"In a few days. I think we'll take in a few of the sights, maybe visit Bandolier and Los Alamos. May as well while we're here." Hays didn't mention there were other issues he may want to look into including a score he'd like to settle for a game leg and a broken pipe.

# Chapter 8

After an old fashioned camp dinner of hamburgers, beans, fry bread, and coffee, Hays asked Deirdre to bring Begay's notebook to the table. While he waited, he lit his pipe, then took out his cell phone and called Anna Begay.

"Hello, Anna, it's Hays. Has Sheriff Kaplin talked with you?" He listened for a moment, then said, "I know, honey, and I'm so sorry. We're going to stay in the area for a few more days but we'll see you before we leave New Mexico. We have things of Evan's we have to return to you." He listened again for a moment and when Anna paused, he said, "Yes, the Sheriff will return Evan's personal effects to you. You know Evan kept a notebook of his searches. We have it, so when the Sheriff returns Evan's things, please don't mention it. I'll bring it to you. We should be back in Albuquerque in three days at most, but if you need me, call me.... Bye, honey."

Deirdre had placed the notebook on the table while Hays was talking and then sat down across from him. He looked at her for a few seconds…. "She's devastated. I think she knew, but nonetheless, she's devastated."

"I could go into Albuquerque tomorrow and stay with her a couple days."

"You could, but I'm certain she has friends and neighbors who will help, and though I don't know for sure, I suspect Evan has family that will be there. Aside from that, I need you here. I'm going to try to make it up to the top of the mesa tomorrow and will probably need your shoulder to lean on as well as Jake's."

"You're supposed to go into the hospital tomorrow to have your bandage changed," said Deirdre.

"I already asked Jeanette and she said she could do it tomorrow before we start out for the mesa. Its not seeping and I think it will be fine with a clean dressing."

Hays opened Evan's book and turned to the last few pages. "There are a few pages starting before the last three he wrote after he went into the fissure that are important, probably more important than anything else in the notebook. Everyone gather around and I'll read them aloud."

Jake sat down and lit a cigarette while Jeanette poured coffee for everyone and then pulled a chair up to the table.

Hays set his pipe against his coffee cup and cleared his throat. "Only some of the pages in his journal are dated but all are numbered. I'm beginning on page 81."

*After my discovery of the cave two days ago, I've come to the conclusion the Anasazi left all their settlements after being convinced to do so by a leader who was in all probability, not Anasazi. Much of what I'm suggesting is conjecture based on pictographs in the cave but I firmly believe I'm right. To prove it, however, will take archeologists and anthropologists on a journey south, to central Mexico.*

*Sometime before they gathered at some unknown central location for their migration, perhaps four or five years, a leader appeared in their midst. The pictures painted on the cave walls show him to be of huge stature for that time, perhaps approaching seven feet, and wearing a headdress with feathers that flowed upward and outward, making him appear even taller. Considering that the Anasazi male stood about five feet tall or in some cases, very slightly more, whoever this visitor was, he must have seemed like a giant or a god, or both. From the drawings, which are remarkably good and well preserved, I suspect he was what we know today as Inca.*

*I am an amateur, but a knowledgeable one, and I would like to set down what I think may have happened to the Anasazi - a hypothesis, if you will, but one that seems to explain the disappearance of a people who inhabited parts of what is currently known as Arizona, New Mexico, Utah, and Colorado. Today, we call this the four-corners area. My premise, or conjecture if you want to call it that, is based on one simple fact: No structured and organized society moves, en-mass, without taking their culture with them; their way of constructing shelter, making clothes, baskets, pottery, etc. If thousands of Anazasi moved to the area of the Rio Grande, for example, we would find ample evidence of that. We have not.*

*There were thousands of inhabited pueblos in what I will call Anasazi land, for lack of a better term. Anasazi is actually a Navajo name meaning ancient enemy or ancestral enemy. At Chaco Canyon alone, there were twelve pueblos and more at other major sites like Bandolier, Mesa Verdi, Canyon De Chelly, and many other locations throughout the southwest. And I've often thought the Mogollon Indians of southern New mexico and Arizona should be included because they disappeared at the same time.*

*Sometime before the migration began, perhaps as long as five years, a delegation of Incas under the command of a powerful and charismatic leader traveled north from Mexico to the land of the Anasazi. Though in itself, this would be unusual, we know there was contact between the Anasazi and the Indians of Central Mexico because of the artifacts found at Anasazi sites. In fact, it has been surmised that the Mogollon may have been the conduit for any trade that went on at the time. Parrot feathers and other South American artifacts have been found at Anasazi sites.*

*My discovery of the cave was purely by accident. I have investigated any number of Anasazi sites and am familiar with what to look for. I had followed my normal routine in the Jemez mesa area as well but found nothing unusual, nothing out of the ordinary. With only two days left to me, I was returning to my camp late in the evening; the sun was just slipping down over the top of the western edge of the mesa when a trick of the light laid a glowing straight line up a steep slope to a smaller mesa atop the one I was on. Approximately twenty feet down from the top there appeared to be a hollow I hadn't seen before. It didn't appear to be a cave but I couldn't tell for sure. I immediately took my notebook from my pack and on a blank page near the front of my book, sketched some notable identifiers which would allow me to return in the morning. The following morning, I returned to where I'd been standing the night before, took out my notebook and looked for the hollow. It couldn't be seen but using the landmarks I'd sketched the night before, I began to work my way up the steep slope. It was a cave.*

*A vertical slab of rock, perhaps twenty feet high, covered most of the entrance, leaving a space slightly more than two feet wide and less than six feet in height. Thinking it could possibly be a den, I checked for coyote or cougar tracks but saw none. Flashlight in one hand and walking stick pointed ahead in case of rattlesnakes, I moved inside. It widened almost immediately and within six feet, I was standing in a chamber of approximately twenty-five feet in length, and twelve feet wide. The ceiling was about eight feet high and the temperature was, like most caves, cool and comfortable. The walls were adorned with numerous pictographs but what caught my attention immediately was an opening, a corridor if you will, at the far end of the room. In size, it appeared slightly wider than the entrance to the chamber I was in but when I shone my light into it, it was deeper and with an left angle to it so that I couldn't see how far it went. As much as I wanted to explore further, I needed more light than was provided by a flashlight and so returned the way I came, back to my camp for my Coleman. Though only at my camp for a few minutes, I had a feeling I was being watched, that primitive feeling that raises hairs on the back of your neck but when I looked in all directions, I could see no one or nothing that might cause it. I returned to the cave, stopped for a moment to light the Coleman lantern, then moved quickly inside. It was then I noticed footprints, not those of an older indian moccasin, but from a modern shoe or boot with cleated sole. They moved in a straight line to and from the corridor at the far end of the room. Someone had been in the cave but it was impossible to tell when because it was sheltered from the elements. It could have been a day, or week, or a year and more. I paused long enough in the first chamber to take pictures of the pictographs and several of the footprints before making my way into the corridor at the far end of the room.*

At this point, Hays paused, took a sip of coffee and relit his pipe. "I will say this: Evan was every bit as much of a writer as he was an amateur archeologist. His journal entries read like a good mystery." After a couple puffs on his pipe, he set it down and continued.

*The passage was narrow, though wide enough that two people could pass each other without difficulty. It ran for about ten feet, angled left and in another ten feet or so, opened to a room much larger than the entrance room I had come from. And in this second room, I found the discovery of a lifetime. Gold! Gold artifacts that from my studies of ancient civilizations, I knew immediately were Inca in origin. So absorbed in what I was seeing, I didn't count the number of pieces but would estimate somewhere in the neighborhood of four to five hundred, most of human form images but many were masks as well. Certainly millions of dollars worth in their present form or melted down. The pieces were laid out against the walls on both sides of the room and I slowly made my way around, not touching, just looking. At the end of the left wall, for a length of three feet or so, was an area where pieces had obviously been laying but were no longer there. The impressions were visible in the fine powdered dirt that covered the floor. Someone had begun removing the gold and intuition told me it was recent, not a long time ago.*

*Finding gold in an Anasazi dwelling was unusual. Finding that much Inca gold was not. The Incas were goldsmiths as can be attested to by records of Spanish conquistadors like Cortes and Pizarro. In Pizarro's case, in the mid 1500s, he had Inca palaces and temples stripped of gold and brought to his furnaces in Cajamarca where it was melted down in preparation of being shipped to Spain. Best estimates put the gold at eleven tons and silver at twice that weight. What was here in this cave was paltry by comparison but in today's market, either as artifacts or melted down, it was worth a fortune.*

*And that's when a startling thought occurred to me. I would have to check my maps but was almost certain this cave was located on Indian land, perhaps part of the Jemez Pueblo. I'm certainly not familiar with the legalities, but suspect the gold artifacts would rightfully belong to them if that were true. My next thought was a logical extension of the first: the cave was being plundered and most likely being melted down for sale.*

*I made my way out of the cave and hurriedly returned to my camp where I made these entries to my journal as I ate a quick lunch. I intend to return to the cave, take pictures, break camp and report my find to the sheriff as well as the archeology department at the University of New Mexico.*

Hays stopped reading and turned the journal face down on the table. "That's Evan's last entry till we come to what he wrote after tumbling into the crevasse on the mesa. Whoever shot him, unknowingly did us and posterity a favor by hitting him at the point where he tumbled into the fissure and onto the ledge. He was returning from his third trip to the cave and must have taken pictures. I assume the camera will be returned to Anna with Evan's personal effects. I'll have to phone her to make sure she puts it in some safe place till she has an opportunity to look at the photos and pass them on to the proper authorities. In the meantime, it might be a good idea to check out the cave and take pictures of our own. We have his sketch of the location and should be able to find it without too much difficulty."

He paused, drawing on his unlit pipe, then finally set it on the table. "The people responsible for Evan's murder will undoubtedly stop at nothing to keep this discovery from being made public. They shot at us, and hit me, simply because we were in the area. I don't think they'd hesitate to kill us all and worry about disposing of our bodies afterwards. Though it might be inconvenient and disrupt what plans they have, they could move the gold to another location in a day or two and if we disappeared, it might be a week or ten days before anyone came looking. They'd have plenty of time.

"This situation could get dangerous and nasty very quickly, so as I see it, we have two options. One, we can contact the sheriff or even the FBI and Bureau of Indian Affairs because the cave is probably on Indian land. Though we'd have some explaining to do about keeping Evan's journal from the sheriff, I think they would overlook it given the circumstances. The second option is to do some investigating on our own, take pictures inside the cave, and gather more information supporting Evan's speculation that someone is taking the gold with intention of selling it. His theory of the disappearance of the Anasazi may be correct as well and that should be passed on to the proper authorities along with his journal and any other related information we might come across. Option number one is safe, sane and sensible. Option number two puts our ass on the line. I think we need to talk about it and decide."

Deirdre smiled at him across the table. "You've already made up your mind, haven't you?"

"Actually, I haven't. There are several constraints if we involve ourselves more than we already have. One is time, or at least time for Deidre and myself. We promised Ben Parker, the fellow who owns the agency we work for, that we'd be back in Ohio in a few days. We could extend that by a couple days without much difficulty but I'd prefer not to. Second, I can speak only for myself and not even for Deirdre. She's kind enough to go along with my wacky schemes most of the time but she has a knack for analyzing situations from a different perspective and I trust her judgment. And third," nodding at Jake and Jeanette, "I certainly can't speak for you two. Whoever killed Evan and is sacking the cave, isn't going to let a few more dead bodies stand in the way of millions, so you'll have to decide which way you want to go. One other thing... If the three of you decide we should end our involvement and contact the authorities, that's what we'll do. I have my own reasons for wanting to continue. I'd like to hammer the bastard who shot me..." He paused, then smiled, "And caused me to break my pipe when I fell."

Deirdre laughed. "I knew there was an ulterior motive. Well, in for a penny, in for a pound. I'm for finding Evan's cave in the morning."

Jake and Jeanette looked at each other, both smiling. It was Jeanette who spoke. "I think we've both decided stay the course, as they say, and for two reasons: Neither of us like to leave a job half finished; we want to see it through to the end. And secondly, its an opportunity to add more information to the history of the Anasazi, maybe even solve the mystery of their disappearance. You can count on us."

Hays was about to reply when he was interrupted by a voice from the edge of the woods.

"Hello the camp!"

It was Leantree. He came from the back edge of the trailer, walking slowly toward the group. "Just thought I'd stop by and say hello if you were still here. Figured you might be gone by now with Begay's body bein' found and all."

Jake started to say something when Hays

broke in. "Nah, we decided to stay a couple more days and enjoy the area. Aside from that, my ass still hurts."

Everyone laughed. Hays picked up his pipe and lit it. He wanted to continue their discussion about the cave and hoped Leantree's stay would be short but didn't want to appear inhospitable. "You want a cup of coffee?"

"Yeah, don't mind if I do." He moved a camp chair up to the table and sat, while Jeanette went to get another cup. "I kinda thought you'd have gone back to Albuquerque by now. Not much to do here unless you visit Jemez Springs or go north to Bandolier. They have nice camping areas at Bandolier."

Maybe it was simply curiosity on Leantree's part, though Hays sensed it was something more. Leantree was fishing for information for whatever reason. Knowing that Begay's body had been found was no surprise. It had probably been on TV and radio as well as word of mouth. News like that spreads faster than a coffee stain on a white carpet.

Leantree took a sip of coffee. "I thought someone might eventually find Begay. No official report yet but rumor has it he was shot. That true?"

It was Deirdre who replied. "He was shot, alright, but that isn't what killed him. Not directly anyway. He tumbled into a fissure in the mesa and fell about thirty feet to a ledge. He died there after several days. Whoever shot him just left him to die."

Leantree shook his head. "Damn... Damn...

Could it have been an accident? Maybe whoever shot him didn't know..."

"Maybe," said Hays, "But I somehow think it was no more accident than me being shot. There's someone who doesn't want anyone poking around on that mesa and I've been wondering why."

"You aim to find out?"

"Might look around a bit."

Leantree finished his coffee and set the cup on the table. "Good coffee. Thank you." He stood up but instead of replying to Hays, he looked directly at Jake. "Ya know, it might just be smart to leave it alone. I sure wouldn't want to see any of you get hurt. Seems like someone's carved that mesa out as their own, what with two people getting shot." He paused. "Well, I gotta be getting back to my place. Thanks again for the coffee."

No one spoke for a moment. Finally, Hays looked directly at Jake and asked, "How well do you know Leantree? I know you've known him for some time, but how *well* do you know him?"

Jake glanced at Jeanette, then turned to Hays. "Well... he isn't family, if that's what you mean. Other than the sense that he's Indian, Puebloan Indian, that is. I've hunted and fished with him. Did some odd jobs with him as well. I count him as a friend but when you come right down to it, I don't really know a helluva lot about him." He took a sip of coffee. "You think he was casting about - trying to find out what we knew and what we were going to do?"

"That's the way it looked to me. Of course, maybe he was just being curious but my gut tells me it was more than that. And his advice about leaving the mesa alone sounded more like a warning than a friendly suggestion."

Jake shifted a bit in his chair. "Yeah, it did to me, too. I'd hate to think he'd be involved in theft and murder but the scent of money can drive some folks around the bend. We'll need to be prepared for anything tomorrow. Might be smart to leave the camp before sunrise so we can be on the mesa at first light."

Deirdre stood up. "We'd better check equipment and weapons. I wonder what the possibility is of something happening tonight?"

Hays cleaned the dottle from his pipe and blew through the stem. "I doubt we'll have any trouble tonight but it might be smart to be prepared. The old handgun under the pillow routine would be prudent. I don't think anyone needs stand guard. What do you think, Jake?"

"I think I'll sleep on the bench seat in the back of the truck. I've done it before and its comfortable enough."

"Good idea. I'll put a handgun under Deirdre's pillow and poke her occasionally through the night to keep her alert."

"Poke her with what?" asked Jake, smiling.

Hays put his pipe in his shirt pocket and laughed. "I ain't goin' there..."

# Chapter 9

Hays smelled the coffee, leaned over and kissed Deidre on the cheek.

"Coffee."

"The aroma drifted in here five minutes ago. I was just waiting for you to notice."

"Aw, take pity on a wounded old man and get him a cup of coffee."

"Wounded? Old? This trailer bounced so much last night, I thought we were going to slide into Jemez Springs. What will Jeanette think?"

"She might think I was exercising my leg."

"Which leg?"

"Well," said Hays putting his feet on the floor, "she might think we were making love. In other words, screwing our brains out."

"You have such a way with words. You get the coffee. I'm going to take a quick shower."

Light was just beginning to show in the clearing as they headed out of camp and up the slope toward the mesa. All were armed and Jake was carrying a pack with first aid kit and some sandwiches Jeanette had made. All carried water and Jake had stowed a couple extra bottles in his pack. Deirdre carried Evan's notebook in a small canvas shoulder bag Jake had given her.

They climbed single file and Hays brought up the rear using his cane for support when needed. When he lagged behind several times, Jake called a rest-halt letting him catch up. When Hays told him to push ahead, Jake said there was no reason to be in a hurry, they'd make it to the top of the mesa about first full light.

Jake was right. They reached the top of the mesa just as the sun was coming up over the mountains to the east flooding the flat table of rock with light. They moved out of the tree line and into scrub brush and broken slabs of rock. Jake slipped out of his pack and set it at his feet.

"Let's take a short break here. The place where Evan camped is about ten minutes walk north." He glanced at Hays with a smile. "We came up by a slightly different route than we did the first time when someone took a bite out of your ass."

Hays took the Ruger 45-70 from his shoulder, stacked it against a boulder, then leaned back next to it. Whether it was the exercise or simply a matter of doing something positive, he felt much better than he had for two days and had walked the last one hundred yards or so without use of his cane. Deidre came over, leaned against the rock next to him and took Evan's journal from her shoulder bag. She opened it, read for a minute and then put it back.

"There are two large outcroppings of rock several hundred yards north of where Evan camped. The first one, off to the left is isolated but the second leads up to a smaller mesa about the size of a football field. I think that's the mesa he referred to and his cave will be in the second one. We don't have the advantage of evening sun as he had but we do have the landmarks he jotted down in his log. The rise to the smaller mesa is about one hundred feet and his sketch shows a flat table rock just to the left of the entrance about half way up, with a spire of rock off to the right and above it. As best we can, we should position ourselves where we think he stood when he first saw the cave and then go from there."

Hays fished in his vest pocket for his pipe, filled it, put it in his mouth, and between puffs he said, smiling, "You know... I really think... you're enjoying this... way too much."

She flashed him a smile. "Mystery, adventure, danger - What's not to like?"

Jeanette, who had been quiet since they left camp, capped her water bottle and laughingly directed a question to Deirdre. "Are you two always like this? If so, I can understand why your love making is a real bang up affair."

Deirdre, blushing and laughing as well, looked at Hays and then back to Jeanette. "Well, he's the noisy one. Truth be told, mystery, adventure and danger kinda sums up our relationship. We compete and love it. It's fun and that's why we love each other so much. Never a dull moment."

Jake cleared his throat. "Ok folks, break's over. Let's see if we can find a cave."

They found it about forty minutes later but without the help of Evan's sketch it would have remained hidden. It was as he had said, a vertical slab of rock, placed at such an angle by either nature or Anasazi, that made the cliff wall appear solid. Over centuries, talus had collected at the base of the small mesa to a height of about twenty feet. The entrance was another forty feet of risky climbing above that. The cliff face wasn't vertical but sloped at a forty-five degree angle and the rock had been fractured by centuries of weather to the point that it pulled loose easily. It took them a half hour just to climb the sixty feet to the entrance. Hays started to enter but as he did, they heard a high pitched bark that sounded like a dog. He looked at Jake.

"Coyote, maybe," said Jake. "Sounded like it but coyotes aren't daytime hunters. Still, it could be." He scanned the area they had come from but didn't see anything. The scrub was a hundred yards off and the tree line another fifty. "I don't see any movement. Let's get inside."

Hays, without saying anything but with raised eyebrow, looked at Deirdre and she said, "Yeah, I feel it too. I think we're being watched."

Hays entered, followed by Deidre, then Jake with Jeanette behind him. As Jeanette started to slip around the slab of rock, a shot rang out and she screamed. Jake spun around, grabbed her arm and pulled her inside. With his arm around her waist, he moved her to the cave wall and yelled for Hays to shine his flashlight on her.

"Are you hit?"

"No... yes... no... I don't know!"

Hays came closer with the flashlight while Deirdre lit one of the lanterns. Jeanette was bleeding from several places on her left shoulder and neck but Jake, looking closely, said, "She's

117

not been shot. Its rock splatter. Take your shirt off, honey, and I'll get the first aid kit."

Rock chips had hit her twice on the neck and three places on the back of her left shoulder. Jake had them cleaned and bandaged in a couple minutes, then turned to Hays.

"I don't mean to be cynical, boss... well, maybe I do, but I think we're in some deep shit here. We're an easy target if we try to go out one at a time, even if we crawl."

"Well, look at the bright side - they can't get in either." He turned to Jeanette. "I'm sorry about this. I should have come in last."

With half grimace, half smile, she replied that doing so would have been worse. He was a bigger target and didn't need to get shot in the ass again. They all laughed nervously, then were silent.

Hays took his cell phone from his belt. "I don't suppose we have a signal here, do we? Maybe we can raise the sheriff."

"Probably not," said Jake. "Look around. Most of this is redrock. High in iron ore, but give it a try."

Hays tried his phone. "You're right. No signal. Probably no better outside but its worth a try if we can get on top of this mesa."

"That's unlikely. We're caught in this goddam cave like rats in a hole. We sure as hell can't go out in daytime and with a three-quarter moon and clear night, it'll be almost like daytime at one o'clock in the morning."

Hays took a couple steps toward the rear of the room. "Let's calm down and give ourselves a few minutes to think it over. We have food and water for at least a day and one thing's for sure, they aren't going to come in after us. Doing that would be as bad for them as it is for us to try to single file out of here. Let's do what we came here for: verify what Evan found and explore the extent of the cave. We have cameras on our cell phones and can take pictures." He turned toward Deirdre. "Honey, let me have your rifle for a minute."

She handed him the .243 and he walked to the entrance, slipping the safety off as he walked. Standing behind the vertical slab and using one hand, he pointed the rifle toward the treeline, fired a single shot, then moved quickly back. Three shots rang out in rapid response, all peppering rock off the entrance.

He looked at Jake. "You catch that?"

"Yeah, either three of them, two with the same caliber rifle and one with a different caliber, or two shooters, one armed with a semi auto."

"That's what I figure. But firing a shot in their direction will make them think were at the entrance, or at least one of us is. They won't try to come in. Let's move on to the second room."

The second chamber was huge in comparison to the entrance area and what Evan had written was true. The number of gold artifacts it contained was truly breathtaking and certainly worth millions, perhaps tens of millions. Hays was no expert but from what he'd seen in museums, the treasure trove appeared to be Incan. In addition to the gold pieces, there were silver medallions and small figurines, blackened with age. In the far corner were beautiful bowls and drinking vessels, all in tact. They simply stood in silence, in awe of the history and wealth that surrounded them.

It was Jeanette who spoke first, not about the

gold but the pictographs that lined the walls of the chamber. She pointed first at the art beginning near the entrance, then with her arm moving in a sweeping motion that traversed the entire room, she said, "It tells a story, and if I'm not mistaken, the story of the disappearance of the Anasazi. The symbols at regular intervals at the bottom of the pictographs give a time frame like a calendar and from what little I know, appear to extend for five years or more. An Incan high priest or god appeared among the Anasazi and over time, convinced them to migrate to Mexico. He was an imposing figure, if the paintings are no exaggeration, who must have stood at least eight feet tall with the headdress shown here on the wall. Without the headdress, he must have been well over six feet, and considering that the average Anasazi man was about five feet tall, the Incan would have had a commanding presence. It will take experts to unravel the whole story but it appears Evan was right."

"If anything is as important than the gold and other artifacts, these wall paintings are," said Hays. "Let's take pictures of everything, the more, the better. And each one of us should put a small piece of this find in their pocket. We can turn them over to the proper authorities when we get out of here but they'd provide solid evidence of what we've seen."

"Speaking of getting out of here," said Jake as he lit a cigarette, "I've been wondering if one of us couldn't belly to the edge of that entrance slab and maybe get a clear shot at whoever has us penned in here. We're high enough above the treeline that they'd be shooting uphill and wouldn't have much of a target, if any."

Hays lit his pipe. "Good idea, Jake. We'll finish up here in a couple minutes and go back to the entrance."

Deidre touched Hays on the arm. "Your pipe smoke."

"What about it?"

"It's moving toward the back of the chamber where those bowls are stacked."

They stood and watched as the smoke moved slowly toward the bowls, curled around them and disappeared.

Hays looked at Jake. "Exit?"

"Maybe. Let's take a look."

The bowls and drinking vessels were stacked against a slab not unlike the one at the entrance, but smaller.

Hays pocketed his pipe. "Let's move these bowls aside and take a closer look at this slab."

Had it not been for the smoke, no one would ever have noticed that the slab wasn't part of the wall. It was more than six feet high and tapered to the left with an edge that fit neatly up against the rock wall. About half way up the stone edge there was a small separation of about a quarter inch and that's where the pipe smoke had curled around and disappeared behind the slab. Hays stooped, took his pipe from his pocket, lit it, then blew smoke toward the edge of the slab. It quickly disappeared through the separation.

Hays straightened up. "Well, its definitely a way out."

"For smoke, at any rate," said Jake, sarcastically.

Hays grinned. "Anyone ever accuse you of being a cynical bastard?"

"Not out loud." Jake tossed his cigarette on the ground and stepped on it. "I meant what I said. Take a look at the slab. It must weigh five hundred pounds if it weighs an ounce and we don't have a pry bar to move it."

"But we both have hunting knives. If we can just pry it away from the wall far enough that we can get four sets of hands on it, we might be able to shift it enough that we can see what's behind it. Maybe it's a way out or maybe not, but we'll never know unless we try."

Hays and Jake, using their hunting knives as short pry bars, managed to move the slab about an inch, just far enough that the group could get their fingers around the edge and pull. Jake had the top followed by Jeanette, Hays, and Deidre on the bottom, kneeling with her cheek against Hays' groin. Just as they started to strain against the rock, she looked at Hays. "Don't get any ideas."

"Ideas of that kind are on hold for now."

Jake barked a laugh. "Jesus, you two! One track minds!"

"It's moving!" Jeanette shouted.

And it was. They pulled till there was about an eighteen inch gap and then stopped. Deidre sat down on the floor of the cave and Jeannette joined her.

"Don't you want to look?" asked Jake.

"No," replied Jeanette. "You look and then tell me. I'm giving my hemorrhoids a break."

"I didn't know you had hemorrhoids."

"I didn't before I came in here."

The beam of Hays' flashlight showed a narrow

corridor that varied from seven to ten feet high, and thirty inches wide, slanting upward at a shallow angle. It also appeared to end about forty feet in.

"Any ledges?" asked Jake.

"None I can see. Why?"

"Rattlesnakes. Check the floor as well before you go in."

"Looks clear. Some faint narrow lines in the dust on the floor."

"Probably mice. Could still mean rattlesnakes. Keep your eyes open."

Hays stepped inside the corridor, took two steps, then stopped to shine his light at ceiling, floor and walls. "The walls seem natural, not manmade. It appears to be a large fracture where one wall, if closed on the other, would fit neatly. Stay put. I'll walk to the end and then return."

Jake watched as Hays walked to the end of the corridor, stopped, turned to his right and shined the light upward. He then walked back, re-entered the main room, picked up a water bottle and drank before speaking.

"Its musty in there and damp toward the far end. There's no doubt that it's a way out because there are hand and footholds in the sloped wall to the right at the far end. It goes up about twenty five feet but to what, I don't know. I couldn't see light coming through from anywhere above so maybe there's another slab of rock covering an exit. If that's the case, I don't know how the hell we'd move it. We'll have to get a closer look."

Jake took his flashlight from his pocket. "Sit on your butt for a few minutes. I'll take a closer look."

Just as Hays had done, he stepped into the corridor, stopped, looked at the walls, ceiling, and floor before walking quickly to the far end. There, he turned right, took a step and disappeared from view. They could hear some scrabbling and grunts.

"I'm climbing the slope," he shouted. "Footholds are deep and close together. Easy to hold onto." There was a pause, some scraping, and then, "Damn!"

They could hear him climb down and within a minute, he was back with the group. "It's a back way out. No doubt about it. At the top of the slope, there's a hollowed out area several feet deep with some stout sticks laying in it. There's a slab that I'm sure covers an opening and the sticks were probably used to push it up far enough to wedge others into the edge to slide the cover back. The problem is that it won't budge. I tried. There may be dirt and growth on top of it or it might be a case of it simply not being moved for centuries. So now what?"

Hays looked at Deirdre, then back to Jack. "We have to try. Is there enough room for two to work up there?"

"Yeah, if we can juryrig something for one of us to stand on. The footholds are only on one side but its narrow enough that one of us could brace his back against the far wall."

"Any pitons in your pack?"

"I think so." Jake rummaged through the pockets of his daypack and found four. "No rope, though. These were only left in the bag because I forgot them."

"OK. I'm wearling a heavy web belt and so is

Deirdre. If you could find some crack to take the pitons at knee level, we can rig the belts in them so a person would be at the same level as the person using the footholds."

"These *persons* are you and me, I suppose."

"You suppose right. If we can gouge out enough around the slab with our knives, it'll either fall on us or we'll be able to wedge sticks through enough to move it."

"Fall on us, more likely."

"Shit, Jake, think positive."

"And what are the ladies on this picnic outing to do while you boys are digging a tunnel in reverse?" asked Deirdre while removing her belt.

Hays picked up her rifle and handed it to her. "Damn! This place is full of cynics today. You and Jeanette go to the entrance, poke your rifle out and fire one round in any direction as long as its downhill, then get back from the opening. There will probably be answering fire. Then come back here. I may need someone to catch me when I fall."

Jeanette laughed. "Ain't going to be me. Two hundred pounds of pissed off Irishman is more than I could handle."

Hays took a sip of water, then sat on the cave floor. "OK, Jake. You go first and lay in the belts. I'll follow when the ladies get back."

A few minutes later, he heard a single shot followed by two returns in quick succession. Sounded like two different calibers, thought Hays, one lighter than the other. So... there's still at least two men out there shooting back. He was surprised they hadn't called for reinforcements.

Then again, maybe their cell phones are as dead as ours.

Jake hollered for him to come up just as Deirdre and Jeanette came back. Hays took off his shirt, laid it on a pack, and smiled as he handed his pipe to Deirdre. "Guard that with your life. Its an old friend." She put the pipe in her shirt pocket and leaned forward to kiss him on the cheek. "Be careful."

When Hays got to the top of the shaft, Jake had already wedged two flashlights into one of the handholds and jammed a heavy stick into a hole at the edge of the cap on the side Hays was standing on. The stirrips formed by the belts were awkward but solid enough if he propped himself against the side of the wall Jake was on.

Jake shifted so he was turned slightly sideways, giving Hays a bit more room. "I've looked it over and it lifts from your side so that's what we have to clear. On my side, there's a bit of a ledge and a corresponding lip on the cover that acts like a hinge. The slab is about three feet long and two feet wide. How heavy depends on how much dirt and debris has collected on the top over the years. If you start with your knife about half way around, angled away from the slab, and work to the other side, I'll keep pressure on it with this staff. Meant to ask, by the way, how's your thigh?"

"Stitches are holding but it hurts like hell. Bearable, though. I didn't think to bring pain pills with me. Anything in your first aid kit?"

"Ibuprofen, I think. We'll check when we get down."

Hays scraped and gouged solidly for twenty minutes, then leaned to his left. "Give it a shove."

Jake turned slightly, bent his legs and pushed upward. There was movement, slight, but movement enough to wedge another stick in the space they'd opened up.

"Let me clear a bit more," said Hays. There's a couple more stout sticks here. Maybe if we both push on it, we can break it free."

"The belts might break."

"If I can get one foot in a foothold and the other on the belt, that might do it. We gotta try, Jake."

Hays worked on the edge for another ten minutes.

"OK. Let's try it." He shifted his left foot into a foothold below Jake's feet and slid the longest stick out of the hollowed out space, jammed it in the hole next to Jake's, then both pushed. The slab lifted straight up, and stopped when it reached slightly beyond verticle, the stone hinge holding it in place. The looked at each other and grinned.

Jake slapped Hays on the shoulder. "I could use a cold beer"

Hays laughed. "So could I, and I don't drink."

"What time is it?"

"Early afternoon, I think," said Hays. "I left my watch in my shirt pocket down below. Why?"

"Just thinking... If its about three o'clock when we get up top, those bastards that have us penned up will be looking into the sun to see us."

"Well, we can't wait in the cave. We need to get out. They might get it in their heads to work around and get on top behind the entrance."

"Yeah. Hadn't thought of that. OK, let's get the women and get out of here."

# Chapter 10

Twenty minutes later, they were sitting in the shade of several scrub juniper trees thirty feet from where they'd exited the cave. The mesa angled up to a point slightly above where the entrance to the cave was located, blocking any view downward to the treeline where the two were who'd been shooting at them.

Jake handed Hays two ibuprofen and a bottle of water. "You have a plan?"

"Yeah. Shoot the bastards."

Jake grinned. "Good plan. How?"

"There's a small clump of bushes near the edge overlooking the entrance. Deidre and I will belly up to it single file then we'll move to each side of it and see if we can spot them. If we do, we'll take them out."

"And what are we supposed to do while you're playing cowboy?"

"You follow us single file and if we get into a firefight, you join in with your Winchester. The reason I said Deirdre and myself is that she has the .243 and I have the 45-70. Both are scoped which should give us a bit of an edge."

"What do you figure the distance is to the treeline?"

"Two hundred yards, maybe a bit more."

"That's a bit of an accuracy stretch for the 45-70."

"Yeah, but if I hit him anywhere, it'll put him down."

"OK, let's do it."

They crawled single file up to the bushes and Hays pushed his rifle into it, taking care not to let the end of the barrel extend beyond the brush. He forced down a couple limbs and looked through the scope.

"I see two, just as we figured," he said in a low voice. "Both are partially hidden, one leaning against that Pin Oak tree to the left of that narrow strip of rock that sticks out from the treeline, and the other is sitting to his left about twenty yards. He's partially hidden behind that cone shaped rock that's about ten feet high. See 'em, honey?"

Dierdre was next to Hays on his left and looking through her scope. "Yeah. I don't think we have a killing shot at either but we can put them down. Which one do you want?"

"I'll take the one against the rock. If I can tag him, it'll keep him from getting back into the treeline. That'll keep us from shooting across each other. Get a good sight picture and then squeeze it off. I'll follow."

Ten seconds later the .243 cracked and Hays' heavy rifle followed almost on top of it. Both men went down but the one that had been behind the

Oak crawled a few feet before he stopped and lay still.

A few minutes later Hays was standing over the man he'd shot when Deirdre called to him.

"Hays, you'd better come here."

"In a minute."

He stooped to look at the man who was unconscious but breathing. Hay's bullet had caught him below the collar bone, inside his left shoulder, and the man was bleeding profusely. He turned to Jeanette who was standing slightly behind him.

"See if you can find something to put pressure on that wound. The way that blood is pumping out, it may not save him but we can try. I don't like doing him any favors but the sheriff might want to talk with him"

He walked over to Dierdre and Jake. The man laying on the ground at their feet was Leantree. He was hit on the right side below his ribcage, through and through, and it wasn't bleeding much. Hays stooped down next to him.

"I kinda figured..."

"Thought you might." Leantree whispered. "I was a bit too nosey last night." He paused, grimaced, then went on. "I tried to warn you before you went into the cave, I barked."

"We heard you," said Jake. "Thought it odd a coyote would be hunting through the day but didn't see any."

"Kinda stupid of me in any case. You'd come this far. Weren't going to stop. But these guys... killers." He coughed. Bright red blood formed on his lips.

Hays turned to Jake. "See if you can raise the sheriff on your cell."

When he looked back to Leantree, he said, "Looks like you have some lung damage. We'll try to get you out of here. I don't know the guy I shot. Where are the other two, Stevens and Chambers?"

"Los Lunas, south of Albuquerque... melting gold. Leastways, that was what they planned." He paused. "Have any water?"

Jake took a bottle from his pack and handed it to Hays who gave Leantree a sip.

"Thanks... Phone service is spotty up here. Dead spot here but three hundred feet in any direction might be fine. We tried calling them when we saw you headed for the cave but no luck... Made a connection but voice was broken."

Jake had been trying to reach the sheriff but shook his head. "No service here. Strange we should have it below at our camp and the other end of the mesa but not on the flat. Hard telling why."

Just then, Jeanette came up behind Hays. "The other one's dead. Must have been pretty busted up inside. Bled a lot."

Hays stood. "Yeah, a 45-70 will do that. Designed for big game like bear or moose. Well, no loss." He turned to Leantree. "I don't think we can get you down to our camp. Jake, you and Deirdre stay here and Jeanette can go with me go back to our camp and raise the sheriff. I'd normally take Deirdre with me but its best there's two here with Leantree and that .243 might come in handy if Stevens and Chambers show up."

The trip back to camp was tiring for Hays. More than once he paused and leaned against a tree. Twice, he tried walking backwards with Jeanette keeping her hand on his shoulder but that meant she had to walk backwards as well and it was time consuming. During one short pause, he commented that he'd like to find a small grassy spot and take a nap. She urged him on, saying he could take a nap once they were in camp. When she promised him fresh coffee and a soft pillow for his butt, he laughed and felt better.

They were little more than half way to their camp when Hays paused again and leaned against a tree. Jeanette, who was following behind, stopped and rested her hand on his shoulder. "Your leg hurt?"

"Like the devil, but I'll be OK once we're in camp and I can sit a bit. I'm going to take you up on that soft pillow. May as well try to raise the sheriff while we're stopped."

To his surprise, Hays made the connection and after a short discussion with a deputy, was connected directly with Sheriff Kaplin. He explained that two men had been shot, one still alive, and that they'd need a rescue chopper. He gave Kaplin the location in relation to Evan Begay's camp. As he and Jeanette started their descent again, it dawned on Hays that he hadn't told the sheriff that just Jake and Deirdre were on the mesa. Well, no matter. The sheriff would find Hays when he wanted him.

They made their camp about twenty minutes later and a considerate Jeanette wouldn't let Hays sit till she got a pillow for his chair. Then she went about making a pot of coffee. When the coffee finished perking, she poured two cups and went to sit next to him.

"This has been the adventure of my lifetime. A week ago, I never could have imagined everything that has happened in a few short days. It it always like this for you?"

Hays smiled and fished in his pocket for his pipe. "No, much of the work of the agency is mundane. Security, mostly, though we occasionally take on some domestic cases. Not often. Lately, however, I seem to have had my share of adventure. I'll be glad to get back to a quiet divorce case, or a review of industrial security for a manufacturing firm." He filled and lit his pipe.

She took a sip of coffee. "That smells wonderful. What brand is it?"

"I blend it myself. Mostly Red Virginia and Aged Virginia tobaccos with a bit of Burley added."

"It smells woodsy and nutty like a wood fire and roasting chestnuts."

"It tastes the same. That's why I like it. Deirdre likes it as well, which is nice."

"You love her a lot, don't you?"

"Bunches."

"Going to get married?"

Hays set his pipe on the camp table and picked up his coffee. "That's the plan, but we haven't set a date yet."

"But soon, huh?"

"Yeah, I think soon."

"That's good. You two are simpatico. You belong together."

"Simpatico... good word. I'll tell her you said so."

Hays took a sip of coffee, set his pipe on the

133

table and leaned his head back on the chair. Within a minute, he was asleep.

An hour or so had passed and he was dreaming. Dreaming he was coming down the hill again from the mesa and a limb from a tree had poked him in the neck just under the right side of his jaw. He heard a muffled scream and a thud, and woke with a start. It wasn't a tree limb, it was a pistol being held against his neck by someone standing behind him. Jeanette was lying on the ground, face down and Milt Chambers was standing just over her holding a handgun. Chambers must have hit her with it because she was bleeding from the right side of her forehead.

Chambers looked at Hays and smiled. "Where are the others?" The gun being held by the man behind Hays, who he assumed was Bill Stevens, pressed harder into his neck.

"Up on the mesa."

Jeanette stirred and Chambers put a boot on her buttocks. "Just stay where you are, honey. You look good in that position." He glanced at Stevens. "I wonder if Indian pussy is the same as any other?"

"We don't have time, Milt."

"Got a lotta time if they're still on the mesa."

Chambers slipped his handgun in his belt holster, reached down and yanked Jeanette's jeans almost to her knees, pulling her panties with them, then lifted her by the waist so she was kneeling with her head to the ground. He unbuckled his belt, dropped his pants down to his knees and said to Stevens, "If he moves, kill him," then moved forward to grab Jeanette by the waist.

Hays heard the slap of the bullet hitting Chambers high in his left chest just before he heard the crack of the Deirdre's rifle. Chambers staggered and went down on one knee, his gun, loose in his holster, fell to the ground. Stevens managed to move a half turn away from Hays when a second shot from Jake's heavier 30-30 rang out and he went down.

Hays stood, pulled the .357 magnum from the holster on his belt, watched as Chambers tried to stand at the same time, and snag his underpants with his left hand. Hays guessed no man wants to die with his balls hanging out, but as Chambers slowly straightened he looked at Hays and saw him smiling. That's when Hays shot him center chest, the bullet tearing through him and taking out bits of spine with it as it exited Chamber's back. Chambers staggered one step backwards and then fell forward, still naked from the waist down. Hays turned, glanced at Stevens who still lay crumpled on the ground, and then moved to Jeanette.

Jeanette had rolled over and though she'd managed to pull her jeans over her hips, was lying still in her back. She was crying. Hays knelt down next to her and without saying a word, lifted her into his arms and held her tight. He was still holding her when Deirdre and Jake came into the camp a few minutes later.

Deirdre stopped beside Hays. "Is she alright?"

"I think so. Nasty bump on the head but she should be OK."

Jeanette pulled slightly away from Hays. "I borrowed your man for a minute."

Deirdre smiled. "That's OK. He likes hugs. Want to make some coffee?"

"Yeah, what I made earlier is cold. I could use something stronger, though."

"There's a bottle of bourbon in the truck," said Jake. "I'll get it." As he walked to his truck, he said to Hays, "That other one is still alive, but just barely. Lung shot. Bubbling. Should I try to patch him up?"

Hays thought a few seconds, then said, "Leave the bastard alone. If he dies, he dies. Is the sheriff headed our way?"

"Should be about a half hour behind us."

"Well, if Stevens is still alive when he gets here, he can take care of him."

Jake retrieved the bottle of bourbon from the truck and gave it to Jeanette.

Hays was standing next to the camp table. "How's Leantree?"

"Still alive when they choppered him out to the hospital. He's a tough old bird. I think he'll make it. We talked a bit while we were waiting on the sheriff. He was hired as a guide by Chambers and was with them when they stumbled on Begay and watched him for a couple days. He said he didn't have anything to do with killing Evan and didn't even know about it till the day afterward because he'd gone into town to pick up some supplies. Chambers promised him a share to keep his mouth shut and give them a hand removing the gold. He saw it as a chance to have money like he'd never had before."

Hays picked his pipe up from the table and lit it. "If he lives, the only place he'll have to spend any money is a prison commissary. He'll probably be charged with complicity or conspiracy, or both. Sad in a way. I kinda liked the old guy."

"Me too. Visions of a lot of money sometimes clouds a man's judgement."

"Visions of anything out of reach that a person wants bad enough will cloud their judgement. By the way, that was a helluva shot you made, hitting Stevens at that distance."

Jake smiled. "Didn't want to be shown up by Deirdre."

"Yeah, but she had a scope and you didn't."

"Under a hundred yards, though. Easy enough for a 30-30. It was Deirdre who spotted what was happening. We were coming down the slope when she stopped me, put a finger to her lips and looked through her scope. By then, I could see what was going on. In a whisper, she said, "I'll take the one with his balls hanging out and you follow up with the one behind Hays." That's what we did. She's a helluva woman. Doesn't mince words."

Hays grinned. "No, she doesn't. You always know where you stand with her... or fall, as in the case of Chambers."

They were drinking coffee, Jeanette's laced with bourbon, when the sheriff, Al Kaplan, came down the slope and into the camp accompanied by two men, a deputy and an EMT carrying a medkit. The expression on Kaplan's face told Hays he wasn't in a good mood.

"Jesus Christ, McKay! A dead Body up on the mesa and two bodies here! I don't know whether to place you under arrest or kick you out of the county." He glanced at Stevens just as he moaned. "Is that one still alive?"

Hays put his cup on the table. "Sounds like it. I thought he might have bled out by now. He was trying hard enough."

Kaplan nodded at the EMT who knelt down beside the wounded man. "You didn't try to stop the bleeding?"

"He was going to kill me till Jake stopped him. I'm not going to do the bastard any favors. The dead one over there with his pants down around his knees was in the process of trying to rape Jeanette when Deirdre gave him second thoughts with a bullet high in the chest. I finished him when he went for his gun."

It was a lie no one could disprove, thought Hays. Chambers' pistol was just a foot from his right hand.

Kaplan looked at all of them in turn, mumbled, "Bunch of goddam commandos," under his breath, then turned back to Hays and stared at him for about twenty seconds. "Got any more coffee?"

"Fresh pot. Bourbon too, if you want it."

"No booze. That's all I'd need. I'm going to have a hard enough time with this mess as it is. From what I gathered from those two," He nodded at Jake and Deirdre, "the shootout on the mesa was self defense and it appears what happened here was as well."

Kaplin accepted a cup of coffee from Hays. "You're going to do two things: break camp this evening and check into a motel. You call me after you check in to the motel. I want to know where you're staying. Then you show up at my office at nine o'clock tomorrow morning. I want all this in writing. If you don't show up, I'll have an APB issued for all of you by ten. Clear?"

"Clear. I think we'd like to see Mrs. Begay this evening. That a problem?"

"Not as long as you're at my headquarters in the morning."

Kaplan turned to the EMT. "He going to make it?"

"Maybe. I've called for Lifeflight. They can land in the clearing. ETA thirty minutes."

He turned back to Hays and paused as he took a sip of coffee. "Just who the hell are you?"

"I told you before, Sheriff, a friend of a friend. I know Mrs. Begay and offered to look for her husband."

"Well, you found him and a lot more. Who do you work for?"

"A security firm in Columbus Ohio."

"Ex-military?"

"Marine recon."

Kaplan glanced at Deirdre. "She ex-military, too?"

Hays didn't quite manage to suppress a grin. "No, just a good shot."

"I should say so. And the rest of this crew?"

"Guide, and his sister who makes damn good coffee."

Hays paused while relighting his pipe, then went on. "We didn't come here looking for trouble but after finding Evan Begay's body and the Anasazi cave he discovered, trouble in the form of these four bastards who were shot today was probably inevitable. I don't run from trouble."

"Apparently not. That cave... Those two told me about it up on the mesa but I didn't see it. They said it was filled with gold artifacts. True?"

"True. This place is going to be crawling with

archaeologists and anthropologists in a few days. Probably the Jemez Indian Council as well. And while I'm thinking of it, these cave robbers were melting gold somewhere in Las Lunas. You'll have to find out where from Leantree, or Stevens if he lives."

"Damn! And I was scheduled to go on vacation next week. You could have just stayed in Columbus, you know."

"Yeah, but you'll be famous. It'll ensure your re-election. Hell, you might even want to run for governor."

Kaplan winced. "No thanks, I just want to make it to retirement.

As they set about breaking camp and packing their gear in the trailer and truck, the lifeflight helicopter landed and picked up Stevens who was still alive, and Chambers body. They finished in short order and were on their way back toward Albuquerque within forty minutes. After Hays commented they had better stay together till after their morning meeting with the sheriff, Jeanette phoned ahead to the Courtyard hotel in north Albuquerque and reserved three rooms.

Hays took his cell phone out. "I think we should all meet with Anna Begay this evening if she's free. I know she'll want to meet you two."

He spoke with Anna several minutes and though the others heard his end of the call, he filled them in. "She says a memorial service for Evan will be day after tomorrow and she will later scatter his ashes somewhere in the Sandia mountain chain. It's apparently what he wanted. The Sandias are sacred to the Navajo. She said she'd love to see us and if we could come by about eight o'clock it would be fine. I told her we'd be there. That will give us several hours to check in to the hotel, wash some of the dust off, and have a bite to eat. Jake, do you have any gun cleaning equipment with you? I'd like to clean Evan's guns before we return them to Anna."

"Yeah, a complete kit. I'll get it for you when we hit the hotel. Been meaning to ask, but when do you plan to return to Ohio?"

"Probably day after tomorrow if all is OK'd by Sheriff Kaplin. I suspect we'll need to make another trip out here for the trial of Leantree and Stevens but that's a ways down the road. Before we go to see Anna, I'll figure out what we owe you both and make out checks. Though this adventure has been technically off the books, they'll be drawn on my company's bank. I'll talk with Anna about expenses. I'm not sure what her financial situation is but we'll work something out. I'll take care of the paperwork end of it when I return to Columbus."

They checked into the hotel, Hays putting all the rooms on his corporate card, and agreed to meet in a couple hours for dinner. Hays and Deirdre had what he called a semi-suite with large bath, room with separate lounge area and a balcony. All the rooms were non smoking but the balcony was equipped with two chairs and a table. Perfect for coffee and a pipe later in the evening.

Deirdre first checked out the bathroom and was peeling off her clothes as she came into the bedroom area. Hays looked up from the bed, smiling.

"Before or after?"

141

"My God, the minute you get in a prone position, you're horney."

"That's not true. The reason I get in a prone position is *because* I'm horney."

"After... Maybe."

"OK. I'll call the office while you're getting sprinkled."

Hays was till on the phone when Deirdre emerged from the bathroom, trailing steam and the aroma of gardenia.

"Right, Ben. I'll tell her... Yeah, probably day after tomorrow, late afternoon. If its going to be later or another day, I'll call. Tell the gang we said hello."

Deirdre, wrapped in a thick robe and a towel around her head, sat down on the loveseat across from the bed. "I take it that was the boss."

"Yep. Ben Parker, the guy who signs our checks. He said to say hello. I filled him in on all the high points and told him I'd have a full written report in several days. Though our being here was the result of a personal request to me by Anna Begay and not a direct request to our agency, he's going to treat it as if it were. I don't think its out of the kindness of his heart. I think he has a not so subtle ulterior motive. He wants to expand, to open an office in the southwest, and I'm sure he's thinking once our part in recovering the gold artifacts is known, it will be beneficial for business. He wanted to know if we'd be interested. I told him I'd let him know in a few days"

Deirdre, who'd been towel drying her hair, looked up quickly. "Are we? I mean, I don't know. What do you think?"

"I really like the southwest and if it were

simply for myself, I wouldn't hesitate, but we're a twosome and I can't make a decision like that alone. We both need to think about it and then talk it through."

"OK. I'll think. You shower."

"And then?"

"I'll think about that, too."

"Want to help me shower?"

She threw her towel at him. "Go get sprinkled."

When Hays came out of the bathroom, towel wrapped around his waist, Deirdre, still in her robe, was reading a copy of Albuquerque Magazine. She glanced up as he bent forward to kiss her on the neck.

"God, woman, you smell good."

She didn't say anything, but reached forward and tugged at the towel which fell to the floor.

"It would appear your interest is in more than my perfume."

He glanced down. "So it would appear."

She got up from the chair and holding his arm, moved him toward the bed which had magically been turned down while he was in the shower. She got into bed and he slipped into bed next to her, his arm sliding around her waist as he nuzzled her neck below her ear. He kissed her passionately and she responded, arching her body slightly.

His hand moved downward to between her legs and he and he followed it, lightly kissing first her breasts, then stomach. He kissed her just above the knees, first one and then the other. She spread her legs and he bent her knees, raised her legs, and began kissing the inside of her thighs.

She quivered, a wave of passion running through her and then she felt his tongue and moaned. After a few moments, she whispered, "Now, Mac, now!"

His full weight was on top of her. She could feel him hard and erect, and she raised her legs and locked them around his back as he entered her and moaned softly, "Oh yes... oh yes..." They moved slowly, then faster as passion took them both, moving now wildly, thrusting, till neither could hold back and they reached orgasm. After a few moments he slid to the side and chuckled.

She looked at him. "What's so funny?"

"Wasted showers. Want to take another together?"

"Yes, but short and no hanky-panky."

"I'll hanky your panky!"

"You just did... Mac, I love you so much."

"I love you too, sweetheart, more than life itself."

At dinner, Hays gave checks to Jake and Jeanette. "That should cover expenses and wages. I included rental for your trailer, Jake." He turned to Jeanette. "Just out of curiosity, have you ever done any bookkeeping or office work?"

"Though I work as several shops, I'm technically self employed, keep my own books and have a filing system to track my regular customers. Why?"

"I spoke with the head of our company this evening and he told me he's serious about expanding his security operation to the southwest. He wants to open an office here and if he does, he'll be looking for some qualified people. There's no rush because it would probably take three to six months to put everything in place, but I thought you and Jake might be interested. Wages are good and it includes benefits."

"Would I be confined to office work?"

Hays smiled. "No, not at all, but the office would need a manager; a job that's critical to all other operations."

Jake set his coffee down on the table. "Would you and Deirdre be part of this operation or would you remain in Ohio? I might really be interested if you two were going to open the new office."

"We've been asked, but like you, would want to think about it a bit. We both like the southwest and since marriage is in our near future, it would be a nice opportunity to start a new life in a new place.

"And not only do I think it would be good for us," said Deidre, it would be fun as well. New home, new furniture, new clothes..."

Hays chuckled. "And a zero bank balance within three months. As much as we like the idea, we still have a lot to consider, but when we decide, we'll let you know." Picking up the bill for dinner, He turned to Jake. "I noticed you brought the gun cleaning kit to dinner with you. I'm going to clean the guns. You two can pick us up out front in forty-five minutes and we'll go to Anna's place."

Hays, carrying a large duffle with the firearms in it, rang the doorbell to Anna Begay's home. Expecting Anna, he was surprised when the door was opened by a tall and rather striking Indian of about forty years old wearing jeans and a western shirt. He opened the door and put out his hand.

"You must be Mr. McKay. I'm Aaron Begay, Evan's brother."

They shook hands and Hays introduced the others.

As they entered the living room, Anna came in, went straight to Hays and hugged him before turning to Deirdre. "I hope you don't mind."

Deirdre smiled at Jeanette. "Not at all. He seems to be quite hugable lately."

Aaron took the bag with the firearms in it and the rest of them moved to the patio at the rear of the house. After they sat down, Deirdre handed Evan's notebook to Anna. "We held this back from the Sheriff and didn't mention it to him but I suspect you'll be hearing from Anasazi experts who may want to see it."

Anna opened the notebook, turned a few pages, then closed it and held it close. "A few minutes before you came, a professor phoned. Sheriff Kaplin contacted the archeology department at the university and they're putting together a team to investigate the site. He wants to meet with me next week and said Evan would be recognized publicly for his role in finding and preserving the cave. I hope so. He would like that."

"He deserves it, Anna," said Hays. "Without Evan, the gold and silver would have been melted down and no one would have been wiser."

Anna handed the journal to Aaron, then turned back to Hays. "Aaron has been a great help. He teaches school on the Navajo reservation near Gallup and has taken time off to be with me. Like Evan, he's always had an interest in archeology but they never found time to take any trips together." She paused, then asked, "Will you be leaving soon?"

"We have to meet with the sheriff tomorrow morning so won't make arrangements till afterwards, but we'll probably leave the following day. Not for publication, but we may be back before long. The owner of the company we work for is thinking seriously of opening an office in Albuquerque. He'd like Deirdre and I to relocate."

"Will you?"

"We're tempted and thinking about it but no decision yet."

They talked for another thirty minutes before Hays said they'd better be getting back to the hotel. He collected another hug from Anna and then told her if there was anything else they could help with, to be sure to phone him, even in Ohio.

They spent the following morning at the sheriff's office filling out forms and writing statements of what occurred on the mesa. They were told they could return in the afternoon to sign the transcribed documents or wait till they were done. They chose to wait and went to a nearby restaurant for coffee and sandwiches. They were still there when one of the deputies came in to tell them Stevens had died following surgery. That left only Leantree who could now tell any story he wanted to in order to cover his butt, including being forced somehow into a situation he had no control over. Hays figured he'd still do time but with a good lawyer, maybe less than if Stevens had lived.

They finished eating, returned to the sheriff's station and signed their statements. Kaplin told Hays and Deirdre they would probably be called to testify but that was months down the road.

Jake and Jeanette dropped Hays and Deirdre off at the hotel and said their goodbyes, promising to stay in touch. When they got to their room, Deirdre sat at the laptop and booked seats with Southwest Airlines for early the following morning. The only seats available were business class but Hays said it was cheaper in the long run than staying at the hotel for another five days or so just to book a cheaper flight.

# Chapter 11

They were getting ready for bed when the room phone rang. Hays set the pipe down that he'd been cleaning and picked up the phone.

"Hello."

"Mr. McKay?"

"Yes."

"This is Aaron Begay. We met at Anna's home earlier today."

"Yes, I remember, How's Anna?"

"As well as can be expected. The memorial service is tomorrow." His voice tailed off.

"I know," said Hays. "I'm sorry we can't be there but we are booked on a flight back to Columbus tomorrow morning."

"That's why I'm calling, Mr. McKay. Is there any possibility you could postpone your return for a few days?"

"Call me Hays, Aaron. Everyone else does except Deirdre who calls me a lot of things, some of which are not suitable for mixed company. Why would you want us to postpone our return to Columbus?"

"A murder was committed near Tohatchi three days ago and my cousin was accused of it. He didn't do it."

"How do you know he didn't?"

"He told me."

"I don't want to sound cynical, Aaron, but someone denying they've committed a murder usually isn't good enough."

"That's what the FBI said."

"Why is the FBI involved?"

"They are in charge when a capital crime is committed on a reservation. Lesser crimes are handled by Indian police and the local counsel."

"Has your cousin been charged with the crime? What's his name, by the way?"

"They're still trying to find him. His name is Hunter Tsosie."

"OK. Where is Tohatchi?"

"Its about thirty miles north of Gallup on route 491. Used to be route 666 but some religicos said that was the devil's number so it was changed."

"You said they were still trying to find him. If he went into Gallup, it isn't such a big city that they couldn't locate him."

"He didn't go to Gallup, he went north into the Chuska mountains. He heard they were looking for him and lit out. His mother told me he'd been drinking with a fellow named John Chee in the afternoon and they got into an argument. Punches were thrown and Hunter got the worst of it. Beat up pretty bad according to his mother. Four hours later, Chee was shot dead while standing along the highway trying to hitch a ride. Police say he was killed by a .35 caliber bullet. Hunter has a Marlin 336 in .35 Remington that belonged to his father. Not that many around and everyone knows he hunts with it."

"Well, what is it you want me to do?"

"I'd like you to talk with him and then talk with the authorities. You solved the disappearance of Evan and they'd listen to you. They won't pay much attention to a Navajo teacher and cousin."

"How could I talk with him? Better yet - where could I talk with him?"

"I think I could find him."

"In the mountains?"

"Yeah, in the mountains. There's a place we used to hunt and fish when we were young. I think he'd go there."

"Look, Aaron, I'd like to help but this is damned short notice."

"Please, Mr. McKay... Hays."

Hays was silent for a few seconds, thinking, then said, "Give me your phone number, Aaron. I'll call you back in thirty minutes or so. I can't promise anything. I'd need approval from my boss back in Columbus. OK?"

"OK, Hays. And thank you."

"Don't thank me yet. I'll call you."

Deirdre, in her robe, was leaning against the bathroom doorframe sipping a diet Pepsi. "What was that all about?"

"That was Aaron Begay." And he proceeded to tell her what Aaron had related about his cousin being accused of murder and asking for their help.

She came over and sat on the edge of the bed. "You'd have to call Ben yet tonight and if he gave his approval, we'd need to cancel our reservations."

"I take it you're in favor of another adventure in New Mexico?"

"I know you are. Whither thou goest..."

Hays smiled. "Bullshit! You just don't want to pack your hat."

"You're right. Call Ben."

After explaining the situation to Ben and emphasizing they could build on the publicity they'd be getting because of the Evan Begay affair and the benefit it would be to a new branch office in Albuquerque, Ben agreed they could take a week and look into the situation.

He turned to Deirdre as he set the phone down. "Don't pack your hat."

Then he phoned Aaron.

"We have a week, Aaron. That's all the time we could get."

"That should be more than enough, Hays, and thank you. Sincerely."

"You're welcome. We'll come to Evan's memorial service and we can talk more afterwards. Can you recommend a hotel in Gallup?"

"The El Rancho. A lot of movie stars stayed there including John Wayne, Katherine Hepburn, and Jimmy Stewart. I think all their rooms and suites are named after movie stars."

"Sounds fine. We'll call them in the morning. See you tomorrow."

When he turned back to Deirdre she was standing about two feet away with her robe open. "Ye gads! A flasher!"

She smiled. "Bed?"

"Bed."